Secret Lives

Ernie has spent most of his eighty years in Parbold, Lancashire. He is married to Madeleine and they have two sons and two grandsons.

Secret Lives

More Tales and Fancies

Ernie Savage

Copyright © 2022 Ernie Savage
Cover photograph by the author

The moral right of the author has been asserted.

Apart from any fair dealing for the purposes of research or private study, or criticism or review, as permitted under the Copyright, Designs and Patents Act 1988, this publication may only be reproduced, stored or transmitted, in any form or by any means, with the prior permission in writing of the publishers, or in the case of reprographic reproduction in accordance with the terms of licences issued by the Copyright Licensing Agency. Enquiries concerning reproduction outside those terms should be sent to the publishers.

This is a work of fiction. Names, characters, businesses, places, events and incidents are either the products of the author's imagination or used in a fictitious manner. Any resemblance to actual persons, living or dead, or actual events is purely coincidental.

Matador
Unit E2 Airfield Business Park,
Harrison Road, Market Harborough,
Leicestershire. LE16 7WB
Tel: 0116 2792299
Email: books@troubador.co.uk
Web: www.troubador.co.uk/matador
Twitter: @matadorbooks

ISBN 978 1800464 384

British Library Cataloguing in Publication Data.
A catalogue record for this book is available from the British Library.

Printed and bound by CPI Group (UK) Ltd, Croydon, CR0 4YY
Typeset in 11pt Aldine401 BT by Troubador Publishing Ltd, Leicester, UK

Matador is an imprint of Troubador Publishing Ltd

To Madeleine and all my friends who urged me to write more

Prologue

January 2002

'It's coming!'

'Well, what does it say?' Edward was impatient.

'Give me a minute,' Angela replied. 'We've had to wait long enough. A few more minutes can't matter!'

'I suppose so. And it was good of you to wait until we all could look at it together.'

In 2002, the 1901 census became the subject of much interest. For some, the fascination was the possibility of finding the famous, whose domestic situations were recorded and which had hitherto been protected by the one hundred year rule. A few of these were still alive. For Angela, Edward and millions of others, it became the anxiously awaited moment when they could discover that little bit more about their ancestors, with the hope, or fear, that skeletons might be found in cupboards. Their search had begun nearly thirty years earlier when Angela and Edward were living in different cities and did not even know of each other's existence. The rest of the group clustered around Angela's computer were either babes in arms or not even born at that time. But all had some familial link to the others and to the one they were trying to track down. As the tension built up, Edward allowed himself to relax; his eyes wandered round the room in *Fairholme*, the rambling house in the East Midlands town of Melcester where Angela and her extended family had lived for several generations. It was very different from the tidy conformity of the house in the Yorkshire city of Leverford, the home he and his wife Mollie had shared for the forty years that they had been married. Here, cracks were appearing in the plaster, the place needed a complete redecoration and there were piles of books and papers gathering dust, but of course such matters were not important to them, he reflected. He glanced across to where Henry, their elder son, was standing, holding hands with Joanna, Angela's niece. It was the relationship between Henry and Joanna, formed when they were at university, that had brought them all together on this fateful day. If Henry had followed his father to Liverpool University instead of Cleadonbridge, they would all have remained in happy ignorance.

For what seemed an almost interminable period they sat or stood in Angela's study at *Fairholme*. She was sitting staring at the screen. Someone coughed. Another yawned noisily. The silence was broken by one of the younger members. 'So, what's there then?'

Rather uncharacteristically Angela swore. 'Oh bloody hell!'

'What is it?'

'The blasted programme has crashed.'

The system was, it transpired, overloaded.

Mollie broke the silence. 'It reminds me of a couplet by… who was it? Robert Frost I think:

*'We dance round in a ring and suppose,
But the Secret sits in the middle and knows.'*

It was seven months before Angela and Edward could return to find The Secret.

Chapter 1

1991

'It's sort of like a commune, Dad.' Henry Simpson, nearing the end of his first year reading Geography in the University of Cleadonbridge, had been invited to spend a part of the long vacation with his girlfriend Joanna at *Fairholme*. Over dinner in the family home he was explaining what he intended to do. James, his younger brother, was away at scout camp, which made it easier. Even as a young teen he wanted to join any activity that Henry took part in.

'I don't think I like the sound of that.' Edward spoke rather pompously. It would be unfair to describe the Simpson household in Leverford as stuffy, but it was conventional and not the least of the reasons that Henry was drawn to Joanna was her unconventionality.

Henry's mother, Mollie, ever practical, sought an explanation. 'What exactly do you mean, dear?'

'Well, there are all the gospel writers, Matthew, Mark Luke and... well the last turned out to be a girl so they called her Joanna.'

'Oh, I see! Good church folk then.' Edward was considerably mollified. 'Catholics? All those kids...' A pillar of the local Anglican parish, he had reservations about the

Church of Rome, but was inclined to feel that any church was better than none. He knew his elder son's adherence to the church was wavering.

'No, no, no,' Henry spoke impatiently. 'They are all atheists. And they aren't especially named after the gospel writers. It was just that William and Mary were twins and were always close. William is Joanna's dad. Actually he's usually called Bill.'

'I see.' Edward spoke carefully. 'I think... could you draw out a family tree?'

'I got Joanna to do one.' He pulled a piece of paper from his briefcase. 'She'd explained, but I couldn't remember the details.' He pointed to the family tree. 'The twins both married, and later decided to buy *Fairholme* together. Well, not exactly buy, it was theirs really, it had been in the family for years, but they made it a joint property, I think. It's a big house quite near the centre of Melcester, and they decided they would live there with any children that might happen. Well, John and Mary, she's Joanna's aunt, Bill's twin sister, of course...'

'Hey, slow down,' said his mother, 'your girlfriend is Joanna. What's her surname?'

'Walker. Now Mary, Joanne's dad's twin sister, married first and had a boy and they liked the name Matthew and then they had another and decided to call him Mark, really without thinking, and then Bill and Susan, that's Joanna's parents, got married, that was when they took *Fairholme* over. Someone joked about the next being Luke because of—'

'I see!' His mother laughed. 'And the fourth one, who isn't John, but Joanna, is the child of Bill and his wife. And would I be right in suggesting that you are quite keen on her?'

Henry blushed.

'Don't embarrass the boy.' Edward spoke quite kindly to his son. 'And you go there on the 15th of August? It'll be quite crowded in that house… four parents, four children…'

'And Angela.' Henry added.

'Who is Angela?'

'Joanna's aunt. She isn't married or anything.'

'I see what you mean about it being a commune.'

'Oh that's only part of it. There are always people around; the boys – well, I suppose I ought to say "men" – Matthew, Mark and Luke – have girlfriends who are often there, well Mark's girlfriend lives with them and then there are refugees and political exiles and such—'

'Good heavens!' Edward sounded rather disapproving. 'But all this use of Christian names for the adults, I do hope you will show proper respect for her parents and uncle and aunts.'

'Dad, they don't use the term "Christian name"; I told you, they're atheists. And anyway they expect everyone to use first names. I met her when she came up to Cleadonbridge and she said I was to call her Angela, not Miss Walker.'

Edward made a noise something like "Humph".

★

Joanna met Henry at the railway station and they decided to walk. 'It's only a hop, skip and a jump!' she had said. 'And it's a lovely day. We can go round by the park.'

Fairholme was a double-fronted late Victorian detached house with a small garden facing Balfour Park. There were basements and attics, so Henry supposed it might be termed four storeys. Seeing that he was gazing in some wonder at the house, Joanna explained, 'The place was new when my great-grandparents, Frederick and Edith Walker, moved here in late Victorian times.'

'They must have been wealthy,' Henry suggested.

'He was one of the textile merchants, a filthy rich capitalist!'

Henry laughed.

Although it was next to the commercial centre of the town, the tide of commercialisation had not yet swept into that quiet side street. Most of the houses, of a similar type to *Fairholme*, were still in domestic use, although many were divided into flats.

The house seemed huge to Henry; the Simpsons lived in a 1930s semi-detached house on a featureless sprawling estate in Leverford. *Fairholme* had a garden but it was very different from the tidy rows of bedding plants in the front garden and the equally tidy rows of vegetables and fruit in the back garden at home. This was, well, he thought, if not unkempt, it was far from being kempt. He smiled; something like that had been in a book he had read.

'What's amusing you?'

'I was just thinking how there are words that seem as though they are opposites, but aren't.'

'Like?'

Henry remembered the original, in a P.G. Wodehouse story. 'Disgruntled, gruntled.'

Joanna laughed. 'Well I hope you are feeling quite gruntled at the prospect of spending a week here. I know another one. Unkempt and kempt. This garden is pretty unkempt!'

Henry didn't say that that was what he had originally thought. Was it telepathy that Joanna had come up with that? 'Actually, I have a feeling that there is a word "kempt".'

'None of us thinks it's important, I suppose. And I guess we think that tidy rows of plants are somehow, well, bourgeois.'

'I suppose I'm... we... I mean me and my parents are rather bourgeois.'

'We'll change all that.'

Henry wondered about the "we". Was it Joanna and him acting together? Or was he to be transformed by the extended family with whom he was to stay?

Angela met them in the hall of *Fairholme*. Joanna's name had meant nothing to Edward: Walker is a fairly common name, but Henry's surname attracted a flicker of interest from Joanna's aunt, Angela.

'Lovely to meet you again, Henry! You did say that your name is Simpson?' she enquired.

'That's right.'

'Really? Joanna, you know your great-grandmother's maiden name was Simpson?'

Joanna did not know and was not really very interested. Nor was Henry, who knew very little about his ancestors.

'Do you know where your family came from, Henry?' Angela asked. 'This grandmother had several siblings, but I've been unable to trace them and their descendants. There are hundreds when you look in the St Catherine's House

Index.' Seeing Henry's bewildered look she added, 'The index of Births, Marriages and Deaths for England and Wales. I sorted out one branch, but that was easy because there were two given names and the surname, Rowlinson, was relatively uncommon.'

'Err, no, not really. Dad did something on the family tree, but I don't really know much about what he found. I think we are the fourth or fifth generation of Simpsons to live in Leverford, but I don't know where we came from before that. I suppose we migrated from the countryside somewhere. That was the case with most people, it can be…' He tailed off, having been about to describe one of the classic models of migratory patterns he had studied as a part of his university course. When he came to know Angela better, he would realise that, rather than being bored by this information, she might have found it fascinating. 'Sorry! I just don't know, except that Uncle Charlie did tell me…' He shook his head. 'No, I can't quite remember.'

'I have a letter sent to my grandmother from a cousin, which says something about Yorkshire. Leverford is in that county, isn't it?'

'For heaven's sake, Angela, let him unpack and settle in!' Joanna cried.

'I suppose so. But if you do remember, let me know. Anyway, Joanna will sort you out. I'll be in the kitchen if you are going to have some tea. I think Mary made some scones the other day, and there's some of that jam that we bought at the Amnesty International stall on the market.'

Henry knew that he and Joanna were to share a room; he also knew that it was quite accepted by everyone that this should be the case; after all they had been lovers, he supposed that was the appropriate word, since halfway through the first term at Cleadonbridge, but he felt uncomfortable with the arrangement. He knew how his father would regard the matter. If Joanna were ever to stay with them something like that would not be tolerated. He doubted whether he would even dare to suggest a secret midnight tryst.

They had a quick passionate embrace in Joanna's bedroom. 'Sorry there's not a double bed, just my own single bed and the Zed bed there, which we'll have to put up later. No!' She pulled his hand away. 'There's all night for that and the next seven nights. We'll go down and have tea and scones. I hope they aren't too stale and the Amnesty International jam isn't that disgusting plum stuff like last time. C'mon!'

'Are you sure that your parents are OK about us sleeping together?'

'Why ever shouldn't they be? It's quite consensual and this is the late twentieth century, not the Victorian era! Oh, I know your parents would hate it, but you've got to be your own man.' She pulled his head down and gently kissed him. 'Tea,' she said firmly, 'and scones and jam!'

In the large kitchen they found a woman of Middle Eastern appearance cooking what appeared to be a dish of that region.

'You must be Amina? I'm Joanna!'

The other woman inclined her head graciously and accepted the proffered hand. 'Very pleased!'

'And this is Henry.'

He also shook hands with Amina and murmured something.

'Hammy and Sammy I told you about, Henry. Amina is with them.'

He knew the men were Iraqi refugees, although he was not quite sure what the circumstances of their exile were. Was Amina their servant or the wife of one of them? Later it transpired that Joanna didn't know either.

'They've got the free run of what were the servants' quarters in the attics and we don't really know what they do there. It's regarded as a separate dwelling. They have to come here to prepare and cook food, that's all.'

The scones were tolerably fresh and the jam, was, well, "interesting" was how Henry described it when pressed. He couldn't imagine what fruit had gone into it; the label had peeled off in the damp conditions of the larder from where Joanna retrieved it.

Amina refused the offer of a scone with a gracious inclination of her head. Henry wondered if it was against her religion to eat Western food. He and Joanna chattered on whilst Amina prepared a meal; she worked carefully, with unhurried movements, smiled if she were addressed but hardly spoke. Henry wondered if she spoke English.

'I need a breath of fresh air!' announced Joanna. As they were about to leave, a short man, of Middle Eastern appearance and with a bristling moustache, entered the kitchen.

He was about to address Amina and then seeing that there were others present, he stopped. It seemed to Henry that he looked right past Joanna; certainly his next remark was addressed to him.

'Good afternoon sir,' he spoke with an almost flawless English accent. 'May I enquire who you are?'

'Oh, don't worry!' It was Joanna who spoke. 'I'm Joanna, Bill and Sue's daughter, and this is Henry, my boyfriend.' She extended her hand.

He took it gently and almost bowed. 'Dr Walker's daughter, of course. I have met your brother Luke and your cousins Matthew and Mark already. It is good to be here with you all.' Turning to Henry he shook his hand more firmly. 'My name, sir, is—'

Joanna interrupted. 'You must be Hammy or Sammy of course.'

The man looked slightly irritated, and then smiled rather wanly. 'I know you find our names difficult. I'm Hammy.'

Henry wondered if Joanna's attitude could be described as patronising. He had been well schooled in PSE lessons at the local comprehensive school he had attended. He speculated whether the private school that Joanna had attended had tried to make its pupils think about such matters. Curiously, it was his very conservative father who had taken him to task about a failure to use names properly. German was not taught at his school, but they had a young German man teaching physics. His name was "Junker" and, inevitably he was known as "Junky".

'The word actually means young nobleman and is pronounced "young hair". It's very rude not to at least try to pronounce someone's name properly.'

★

By dinner time the next day, Henry had more or less sorted out the various ramifications of the present inhabitants of

Fairholme. Luke bore a strong physical resemblance to his sister Joanna, so that was easy. Both had dark and rather wayward hair. He was almost sure which of the cousins was Matthew and which was Mark. They were not very like each other, but somehow seemed interchangeable, like Rosencrantz and Guildenstern, he thought. He and Joanna had been involved in a University Dramatic Society production of Stoppard's play; they had respectively been Hamlet and Ophelia, minor roles in *Rosencrantz and Guildenstern Are Dead*, a fact they downplayed. Indeed Joanna had told several people that they played Hamlet and Ophelia, without mentioning that the play was Stoppard's rather than Shakespeare's. It was more from a sense of fun than a deliberate intention to deceive.

The dark and wayward hair had been inherited from Susan, the mother of Luke and Joanna. She was in charge of the meal. 'Now I think you are going to like this, you kids.'

'What is it?' Matthew sounded rather suspicious, or was it Mark?

'Now Mark!' His aunt spoke with mock severity.

Right, thought Henry, Mark is the one who is taller, I think. So the youngest, I mean the younger, is the older, I mean the bigger.

'I'm sure it will be delicious.' This was from Mark's girlfriend, Alicia. 'Your mother's cooking is excellent.'

Susan was continuing. 'Well, it's bean stew with—'

She was not allowed to continue. In unison and almost as if rehearsed, the four younger members of the household chorused, 'If it's been stew, what is it now?'

Henry was surprised. That sort of thing seemed to be more appropriate to Form Four.

'I shall ignore that. Henry, you shall have the first helping. I hope Joanna is looking after you properly.'

'Yes thank you, err… Susan.' Henry still found it difficult to address the adults by what, as he admitted to himself, he still thought of as Christian names.

Angela broke into the conversation. 'Have you had any further thoughts about your family's origin, Henry?'

'I did remember something. My uncle goes through a sort of litany of his ancestors, who are I suppose mine too: Charlie, Freddie, Jimmy, George—'

'Wait a minute, let me write it down.' She produced a small notebook and a pen from her handbag. 'Now, say it slowly.'

Henry repeated it.

'He's starting with himself, Charlie?' Henry nodded. 'So,' she counted on her fingers, 'your grandfather, great-grandfather, great-great-grandfather… all men, so the name Simpson throughout. My great-grandfather and indeed his father were both George Simpson. Have they always lived in Leverford?'

'No, I know that someone, I think it was "Jimmie", he came from somewhere else.'

'But you don't know where they came from?'

Edward shook his head.

'Going back another generation, I've found Margaret Rowlinson and she—'

'Give it a rest, Angela,' cried Mark.

The stew was followed by a fruit tart.

'Sorry it's not home-made,' said Susan, 'but I've been busy with the Support for South Africa group we have here. We need to maintain pressure to ensure the ending of apartheid.'

'What is happening in that country?' Henry asked.

'The AWB are on the rampage and if we aren't careful there will be an even more rigorous apartheid enforced. But right now it's a matter of whose turn is it to do the washing-up?'

'Err...' Henry asked hesitantly, 'what is the AWB?'

'Afrikaner Weerstandsbeweging, a white supremacist group in South Africa.'

'We did the washing-up yesterday,' said John, who had sat quietly in the corner.

'It's Thursday, so it must be Joanna and Luke,' Susan spoke authoritatively.

Henry stood up. 'Well, if Joanna is doing it I must help her.'

'OK, lover boy.' Joanna produced a tray from under the dresser. 'Start stacking these ready to take into the kitchen.'

The kitchen was in the basement. Henry supposed it must have been where the servants worked, though they slept in the attics. The fittings looked as though they might have been new when, what was he called? Mr Walker moved here with his bride in late Victorian times.

The dishes were quickly washed, dried and put away. 'So,' asked Luke, 'are we off somewhere?'

'Well I feel like a night out somewhere,' said Joanna. 'Not that there's much in this town. How about you, Henry?'

'Well, what is there in this town?' he laughed.

'There are lots of pubs,' suggested Luke. 'We could gatecrash on Matt and his mates in the *Van Dyke*.'

'Oh I'm not sure about that, one of his mates might want Henry.' Joanna put her arm around her boyfriend.

'Err…' Henry was confused.

'My cousin Matt is gay and the *Van Dyke* is a gay pub,' explained Luke.

'Oh.' Homosexuality was not something Henry had any real understanding or experience of. He knew it was said that some of his fellow students were gay and that they frequented certain pubs in Cleadonbridge. He was not sure where they were and he had never tried to find out. He knew his father's views on the matter and his worry that one of his sons might turn out to be… how had he described them in that convoluted chat they had? He had not used either the clinical "homosexual" or a slang pejorative term such as "queer". 'Of course,' Edward had said, 'they are to be pitied, and we would not want to have them censured by the law, as it used to be, but…'

Aloud Henry said, 'I've never been in a gay pub.'

Joanna joined in, 'Why would you? And it's not fair to Matt if we go in there. It's a sort of sanctuary for them, even a place of asylum, like this house is for our Iraqis.'

'But surely,' Henry put in, 'they aren't persecuted nowadays. It's been legal since… oh, I dunno, before we were born I think.'

'1967 saw the decriminalisation of gay sex but only if the two were over twenty-one and there is still not full equality,' Joanna spoke forcefully.

Henry was taken aback. 'You seem to know a lot about it.'

'Matt is my cousin and really more like a brother and we all look out for each other in this place; I was the first one he came out to, when he was twenty-one and I was only fifteen. We like to pretend we are liberal and free-thinking but it's not always quite so.'

Henry recalled their attitude to the Iraqis.

'John and Mary were not fully accepting, as Matt feared. Oh they've come round now of course and he has had boyfriends round here and they have been welcomed.'

'I cannot imagine how my father would react if my brother James turned out to be gay.'

'How old is he?' asked Luke.

'Thirteen.'

'Well, time will tell. If there is any sort of issue, we'll help you all we can.'

'Time? If we don't get off soon they'll be calling "Time gentlemen please!"'

Eventually they ended up in an ordinary city pub, mercifully free of fruit machines and piped music. Several of the younger men and women who were there seemed to know Luke and Joanna; Henry was introduced to them. Later, Mark and Alicia arrived. It was all very friendly and rather low key, although Henry was a little ill at ease, knowing that he and Joanna were to sleep together. He somehow imagined Bill as a wrathful father arriving and demanding… demanding what? That he should marry his daughter? He giggled at the thought.

'What's funny?' demanded Joanna.

'Nothing really. I'll tell you later, when we are…' He whispered into her ear, 'alone.'

*

The few days passed pleasantly enough. There were a few visits: one was to the city museum, another was a trip into the countryside; sometimes just him and Joanna, sometimes with some of the other younger members of the family. On other occasions her parents or uncle and aunts came. One never knew who would join a group. Then of course he and Joanna were together at night, though their lovemaking was somewhat uncomfortable on the single bed. He soon forgot his reservations about this and they were able not only to enjoy the pleasures of sex, but to laugh at the difficulties. He was sad to leave *Fairholme* and return to Leverford from where in a few days he, with his parents and James, were to leave on a continental motoring holiday.

*

On his return Henry mentioned the conversation about genealogy to his father.

'Well, as a matter of fact we came from that part of the world. Your great-great-grandfather, James, was born in Melcester and his brother, George I think his name was, remained there. I found out the details from the census. Why do you ask?'

'Angela wondered if we might be related. Her grandmother, so Joanna's great-grandmother, was a Miss Simpson. There was another branch she mentioned, a more unusual name, like Robinson, but it wasn't that.'

'Rowlinson?' his father asked.

'Yes that's it!'

'Oh really?'

If Henry had been a little more perceptive he would have noticed his father had become paler, but at this moment his brother burst in. 'Who's for a run then?' James, who had eaten too many sweets and other unsuitable foods, was having a fitness drive.

'Good idea, brother! Dad?'

Edward shook his head.

'Just going for a quick run round the park, Emandee!' Their sons called their parents by the initial letters of M and D for Mum and Dad. The door slammed behind them.

After they had gone Edward went to find Mollie in the kitchen. 'Apparently Joanna's great-grandmother was a Miss Simpson. And…' He paused dramatically. 'She mentioned a Rowlinson. If she's a Simpson of that generation and there is a Rowlinson connection she could be a descendant of Albert, and we and Uncle Charlie could be liable for goodness knows how much…'

'Edward dear, what are you talking about?'

'Don't you remember? It all started nearly twenty years ago when we were at Otterwood Hall…'

Chapter 2

1973 & 1979

'Edward! That's hardly a word to use in front of your son and heir.'

'He's behind me! And anyway, he's only a baby; he can't understand what we say.'

'That's not the point,' rejoined Mollie. 'Children imitate what they hear. And anyway, William is more commonly known as "The Conqueror".'

The young Simpsons were visiting Otterwood, a stately home near Leverford. The house was Georgian and was full of furniture of that period, but it was built on the site of an earlier mansion. Somewhat incongruously in the music room was hung an elaborate family tree which showed the descent of the family who owned the place; they claimed to be in a direct line from William, Duke of Normandy, or "The Bastard", as Edward had termed him. Henry, the "son and heir", was just old enough to be carried around in a Papoose Carrier and had begun to take a real interest in his surroundings, at least so his fond parents believed.

'Could you do one like that?' Mollie asked.

'A family tree? I suppose so. How far back could we go?'

'Uncle Thomas has drawn one up for our side of the family. Is there anyone on yours who has? He's got back into the seventeenth century. We appear to come from a long line of peasants.'

'It shows!'

For a reply Mollie stuck out her tongue at her husband, much to the surprise of another visitor to the house.

'Well, one was done years ago when Maggie Powell died.'

'Who was she?'

'Née Simpson. She died intestate about 1951. She was quite wealthy; her husband, who died before her, was an industrialist; probably, being in this city, textiles, though I don't actually know. Anyway, the estate was divided up between Dad, Uncle Charlie and someone on her mother's side. It was enough for Charlie and Clara to buy *Wuthering Heights*.'

'I remember now; you did explain it all to me. What a ridiculous name that is to give to an interwar villa! I suppose it's rather a grand house and it is near Haworth, but it's more like *Thrushcross Grange*.'

'Dad spent most of his share before he died, and I have no idea of even the name of the person on the other side who inherited.'

'The other side?' Mollie rolled her eyes in mock horror. 'I didn't think that ghosts could inherit!'

'Ha, ha.' Edward was not amused. 'Her mother's side; she was... oh, I forget. I don't know if I ever knew.'

★

But Edward's interest had been aroused and it was further stimulated because he wanted to be able to demonstrate to their son that the Simpsons, Edward's family, were of a higher social class than the Daltons, Mollie's family. He was rather a snob; later his wife was to suggest that it seemed to run in the family. The family tree that he drew up was based on what little was known among the members of the immediate family. His Uncle Charles lent him the one drawn up when Maggie Powell had died in 1951 and he filled in some details from a study of the trade directories and the 1871 census of Leverford, both of which were in the local library.[1] Their family had lived there for many years; Henry and his younger brother James were the fifth generation to live in the Yorkshire mill town. The first was another James, who set up in business as a pharmacist somewhere before 1871. From the census he discovered that James came from Melcester in the East Midlands. The trade directories from the late nineteenth century and into the twentieth century showed an increasing number of pharmacies across the city owned by J Simpson & Co.

Edward's promotion to head of the geography department at one of the comprehensive schools in the city, and family affairs, meant that it was some time before he went to Melcester, where he spent several days in the record office, which is housed in the former library of the town. The search room is a nineteenth century library, lined floor to ceiling with books and research materials. A winding cast iron staircase connects the galleries with the ground floor. The books and materials seemed to be of a similar age to the galleries and Edward did not see any being removed for

---

1 See the family tree on page 173.

consultation. At the enquiry desk, in a sort of appendage to the room, the archivist staff sat, issuing application forms and materials. Many of the records were on microfilm which needed to be wound on and sometimes he wound on too far and the film slipped. His searches took some time.

Various earlier censuses and church records enabled him to piece together something about his ancestors. James, his great-grandfather, had a brother George who was the father of Maggie. An index had been drawn up for the 1871 census, so finding the Simpsons was easy. They were living at 8, Clarence Villas in Melcester. He had discovered that Maggie, who was not yet born, had a brother not included in the settlement of the estate. Two other siblings, Lillie and George Clarence, were included on the family tree drawn up by Uncle Charlie but they had died before Maggie and had been childless. However, there was also Albert, who was born in 1866.

He had asked for church records to try and find baptisms and marriages. Having drawn a blank, he swore softly, sighed and sat back.

'What's the problem?' The speaker was a woman of about his own age who was sitting at the next reader. She wore casual clothes of the type that later would be called, rather absurdly Edward thought, "ethnic". Her hair was long and arranged in a braid on the top of her head. Her perfume, which he caught as she leaned across, was, he thought, rather earthy.

'I can't seem to locate an ancestor. I know he exists from the census but unlike his siblings there is no record of his baptism or of his parents' marriage.'

'Have you tried the BTs?'

Edward was baffled. 'The BTs?'

'Bishops' transcripts. They are often more complete than the actual parish registers. I've used them a lot.'

'How far do they go?'

'They began towards the end of Elizabeth's reign and continued until about the middle of the nineteenth century. None were done during the Commonwealth of course.'

'The one I cannot find was born in 1866 so wouldn't be on them then. But, wait a minute…' Edward scrabbled through his papers. 'Of course, he wasn't born in Melcester but Charnborough.'

'How did you find that out?'

'1871 census.'

'I see.' She paused. 'Err, my father's family came from Charnborough. I have some interesting information on the place,.' Ahe paused again. 'At my house.' Her tone was positively seductive. She drew her hand seductively across her face and onto her breast.

'Ah mon Dieu!' Edward breathed silently. He had been told that whereas to utter the words "My God!" was breaking the third commandment, the French usage was acceptable in that country. Aloud he said, 'It's very kind of you, Miss, Mrs…?'

'My name's Clarissa, Clarissa Smart. You can come round and we can have a spot of lunch and then…' She raised her eyebrows in a meaningful way.

Edward cleared his throat. 'Well, I need to get on. I have a train to catch later, back to the wife and kids in Leverford. I've got a sandwich that I was going to eat in the garden outside.'

'Are you sure?' Clarissa seemed insistent.

'Quite sure. And now I'll have my lunch... actually I need to go to the loo.' Edward realised that as it was only 11.30 his having lunch would be a feeble excuse, but he needed to escape. Safely in the toilets he breathed a sigh of relief. He believed in a fairly strict moral code, but he also believed that a man should be courteous to a woman. He didn't know whether she wanted to seduce him; perhaps she was simply lonely and wanted a chat, though her manner had suggested otherwise. He remained in the toilet for as long as possible and hoped that on his return to the search room Clarissa would have gone.

She had not. 'Well, it's a bit early for lunch but I've reached a convenient place to stop and I need a breath of fresh air.' He swept up his things and walked out without a backward glance. Thankfully she did not follow and he was relieved to see her passing the gardens and disappearing down the street.

After lunch he resumed his search. If Albert was born in 1866 in Charnborough it seemed most likely that his parents had been married there, but there was no record of such. He then speculated that there was some family connection to Melcester; the earlier censuses had shown that the Simpsons lived there.

'Aha!' he almost shouted. 'Here we are!' The other people in the search room glared at him. He reddened, reflecting that an audible comment had led him into the embarrassing situation with Clarissa. The marriage register for the ancient parish church in Melcester gave July 20th 1867, George Simpson, bachelor, a grocer... married Margaret Rowlinson, spinster... no occupation given. So then... wait a minute, he consulted his notes. Albert was born the year before, 1866.

Perhaps someone had got it wrong; he double-checked everything and went back over other branches of the Simpson family including records of business activity in the trade directories.

It was not until the next day that he found the listing of the birth in the civil registration... Albert Rowlinson born in the first quarter of 1866. Almost certainly Maggie's missing brother. Now if he had been baptised it would have been in a church in Charnborough. But he drew a blank there, trying all the Anglican churches in that town and even the principal Methodist church.

He walked up to the enquiry desk and addressed the archivist, a young man whose long hair was drawn back in a ponytail, a fashion of which Edward did not really approve. 'Excuse me; can I get the actual birth certificates for an ancestor?'

'Hey, yeah, but not here. You need to go to the registrar's office in Northfield Road.' He described the route.

The instructions were clear and within quarter of an hour he was outside the building, a modest nineteenth-century terrace house. For a fiver he was able to collect the certificate: Albert Rowlinson... son of Margaret Rowlinson... No occupation was given and the space for father's name and occupation was also blank. Clearly he was illegitimate, yet George married Margaret a year later.

'Thanks.' He handed his money over and prepared to depart. A sudden thought stuck him. 'Are Clarence Villas near here?'

The registrar's instructions were not as clear as those

he had been given by the archivist. 'Yes, just round the corner, well, two corners – left out here then right and it's off that road on the right.'

Edward left, trying to remember that. He was helped by the fact that the directions had been accompanied by various waving of hands. Even so he had to seek further help, but eventually he found it. The villas were substantial mid-nineteenth century detached houses and were still in good condition. George Simpson must have had a fairly good business as a grocer. It was a pity that he had not thought to bring a camera, but one of the houses was for sale. He noted that the estate agent's office was in a street near the record office and so he made his way there. He asked for details and was given a sheet which had a small photo of "the property", as they called it.

As he collected his things together, before leaving to return home, he realised what must have happened. Margaret must have been sent away to Charnborough, for he had found her in the earlier censuses living with her family in Melcester. They were obviously quite well-to-do. Perhaps they had given George some support to enable him to set up in business, if he would take their daughter off their hands.

*

'Well?' Mollie greeted him on his return. 'Have you discovered anything scandalous or salacious about your nice middle class ancestors in the Midlands?'

'Sort of.' He decided not to tell her about what might have been scandalous and salacious about himself.

The incident with Clarissa on the previous day was too embarrassing to relate.

'Oh really? Tell me more. At least,' there was a wail from their younger son upstairs, 'when I have sorted James out. Put the kettle on; we'll have tea. There's a casserole and a couple of baked potatoes in the oven. We can have that later.'

Over tea he explained. 'I found them in the 1871 census. Quite a nice house it seems near the centre of Melcester, Clarence Villas.' He fumbled in his briefcase and read from a piece of paper: 'Stunning six bedroom house with beautiful kitchen, very close to the university. Six large bedrooms, two good-sized bathrooms. Beautiful kitchen. Spacious lounge and a large garden.'

'Is teaching too much for you so you have decided that you are going into the estate agent business?' enquired Mollie sarcastically.

Edward laughed. 'I walked out to see what it looked like, but as I hadn't thought to take a camera, I popped into the estate agent's and got the details on one that was for sale. Not theirs but similar.'

'How much is it going for?'

'£5,950, a lot more than a hundred years ago. Anyway, George and Margaret lived there together with their kids, Albert, Lillie and George Clarence… odd that they gave him the name of their road.'

'Perhaps they owned the road if they were wealthy,' Mollie put in.

'Unlikely. Anyway, the infamous Maggie, as we know, wasn't yet born, so I started looking at church records, to see when and if she was baptised.'

'And was she?'

'Oh yes. On the 31st of May 1874. She was born on the 12th. I found that from the birth certificate, which cost me a few quid. So they were fairly prompt in bringing her to the font.'

'That isn't always the case. One of my ancestors had neglected that; after four babies she died, but the second wife made sure that they were all baptised. So you'd need the birth certificate as well?'

'Yes, but at first I couldn't find the date of birth of Albert, but I did find his parents' wedding, which was in 1867; I found it in the church records, C of E again, and then I spent yet more money on the marriage certificate. George Simpson, grocer, and no occupation given for Margaret Rowlinson, the bride. The registrar in Melcester was very helpful. *But…*' He laid stress on the last word and paused dramatically.

'So this is the scandalous or salacious discovery. Go on.'

'Albert's age in 1871 is five; he was born in 1866, but his parents only married in 1867!'

'It happens… who was the father? Was it George?'

'I dunno. I saw that he was born in Charnborough, according to the census, so looked for the birth of an Albert Rowlinson. I found him; he was the illegitimate son of Margaret who married George the following year. I wonder what happened to him?'

'Who? George or Albert?'

'Albert. He's not on the family tree drawn up for probate; he may well have died. A lot did die in infancy. But I looked through the deaths and found no one called Albert Simpson or Albert Rowlinson of the right age. There were scores of Alberts – it was only just after the death of the Prince Consort, of course.'

'Was his name given in the census as Albert Rowlinson or Albert Simpson?'

'Simpson, but there were no formal adoption procedures in those days; I checked, he would legally be Albert Rowlinson.'

'Did you find out about… what did you say the name of the mother of Albert and the others, including Maggie, was?'

'Margaret Rowlinson; her family seems to have been quite wealthy, involved in textiles, both the manufacture of cloth and the making of garments.'

'Margaret must have been quite a disappointment to them. She'd be regarded as "soiled goods". Was George a good catch for her?'

'Well, he wasn't a pauper; Clarence Villas, as you see,' he waved the piece of paper, 'are quite substantial.'

'What about George's ancestors? Of course they are your ancestors too… were they wealthy?'

'Not especially, as far as I could find. Middle bourgeoisie, shopocracy, for the most part, but the better sort of shops. We'll have to wait for the 1881 census to see how he made out later, though we're more interested in his brother, James, who is my great-grandfather; he moved to Leverford. I was going to look in the trade directories for George, but I was interrupted. It's very confusing as there is a George in each generation.'

'"High class grocers", like those on Jenkins Road where we shopped.' Mollie was talking about the area of Leverford where she grew up and subtly reminding her husband that her family were not paupers. 'The low class shops were on Travis Road. Mum would never patronise those and Grandma was even more dismissive of them.'

Mollie's family had lived in the inner city hanging on as one of the few middle-class, white families in an area increasingly occupied by immigrants from the Indian subcontinent. She and Edward had met because, although his family had fled to the suburbs not long after Edward was born, they continued to attend St John's Church, until it closed, not long after Mollie and Edward had married there in 1971. Mollie's parents later moved into sheltered accommodation in a village on the edge of the conurbation, not far from the sprawling 1930s private housing estate where their daughter and her husband bought a house.

*

Edward and Mollie pursued their search for ancestors, seizing time off to visit record offices when they could take time from their work, family and social commitments. Albert and his siblings were, for Edward, a mere sideline as he was not descended from them. By diligent effort he was able to push back to the sixteenth century, at least with some of his ancestral links. As he ruefully pointed out, 'You have two parents, four grandparents, eight grandparents and so it goes on, doubling every generation. With there being about three generations each century, my finding this lot,' he waved the paper on which he had drawn up a family tree, 'Hugh Brandholm, farmer, and Mary, his wife, are two of about a thousand ancestors of those two.' He pointed upstairs to where Henry and his brother James were asleep.

'Of course that is on their father's side,' pointed out his wife. 'If you take my lot as well... it's a never-ending task, although of course I am now exploring sidelines that Uncle Thomas didn't venture down.'

'Did you discover anything on the sidelines today?' asked Edward. The earlier families came from different areas, which meant they needed to visit different county record offices. That, together with the need to juggle childcare, meant they pursued their research at different times.

'I thought I'd found a case of bigamy.'

'Oh ho! But it wasn't?'

'No, it was rather a disappointment. I found Hugh Cartlett marrying a Jane Burrow in Arkenthwaite, a little village on the fringe of the Lake District, in 1855. Jane was a cousin of my great-grandmother, born in 1836. So I did a search on the census for 1861. Fortunately, it had been indexed and I found that Hugh was in the town, married to a woman called Elizabeth.'

'But it wasn't bigamy?' Edward asked.

'I found their marriage in the main church of the county town; she was Elizabeth Davies and they had married in 1859. She was a spinster; he was a widower. I checked the village church registers and poor Jane had died less than a year after she and Hugh were married.'

'How sad!'

'Even sadder was the fact that a few days after her death their daughter Margaret died aged only six days.'

'Childbirth was hazardous in those days. You can't blame Hugh for wanting to leave Arkenthwaite. I wonder if the illegitimate Albert may well have died in childhood. We only know he was alive in 1871 and not around to inherit his sister's millions in 1951.'

'Perhaps he might appear out of the mists of time and claim his inheritance?' suggested Mollie.

'Hardly, he'd be over a hundred now, although I suppose he might have had kids. But I'm also baffled by my great-grandfather.'

'In what ways?'

'Well,' Edward dug out a sheaf of papers on which he had written his notes, 'the business continues with the chain of shops in Leverford and one out in Shedford, well into the twentieth century. Of course it all ended when my grandfather died quite tragically at the age of forty-nine.'

'So? Didn't you tell me that your grandfather took over after James's death? They'd want to keep the name.'

'But…' Edward paused dramatically, 'I know from what Charlie said that after James's death, Charlie's father, my grandfather, Frederick, took over and he is listed as managing director in the trade directories and his house is given.'

'16, St Andrew's Terrace, that house you showed me, where your grandmother lived until her death?'

'Yep! But there is no house shown for James and I cannot find any record of his death anywhere! I've trawled through year after year of the St Catherine's House death records.'

'Perhaps he went to Australia?' Mollie suggested.

'Humph!' was Edward's only response.

Chapter 3

1976

In the quest for her long-lost cousins Angela had arrived at a long stone terraced street in Brungerley, a mill town in North East Lancashire. She supposed that when it was built in the late nineteenth century, these houses had been for the rising middle class. The houses were tall and there were small front gardens; some had bay windows. She reached number 159 and pushed open the gate with more hesitancy than was usual in her actions. She liked to imagine herself decisive and forthright, though others used different adjectives. Her twin siblings, William and Mary, had labelled her "bossy" when, in the dark days of the 1940s, she had taken charge of their meagre ration of sweets and in other ways organised their lives. Father was in the army; after Dunkirk, Mother had chosen to enlist as a member of the Land Army, leaving them in the care of Grandma, but she was frail and Angela at four years old felt responsible for her brother and sister. Mother had died when Angela was fourteen and the twins were twelve; their father was quite useless; Angela was in charge.

The gate was rusting and the flags in the short path up to the foot of the steps of the front door were cracked.

Dandelions poked through these cracks and she noticed lily of the valley making its way from the small flower bed on the left and attempting to colonise the right hand bed among some daffodils. There had been snowdrops earlier, she noted. This tiny plot had been cared for. From the voters' list Angela knew the name of the person in the house was Jean Mason. But was she *the* Jean Mason?

She rang the bell. After what seemed a surprisingly short time, the bolts were drawn back and the door opened. Angela had decided that the promptness of the response precluded its being a lady close to her eightieth birthday, but the woman who opened the door seemed to be about that age. The clothes were old-fashioned, but her grey hair had recently been styled and her manner suggested a woman who was in full possession of her senses. Angela had feared the possibility of a woman long sunk in senility.

'Yes?' The tone was neither hostile nor welcoming.

'Mrs Mason?' If she was "Miss" then it was not "her" Jean Mason.

'Indeed it is! Now if you are selling something… Miss, err…'

Angela recovered something of her usual assertiveness. 'Angela Walker.' She extended her hand. 'Good heavens, no. I'm not trying to sell anything.' She forced a laugh. 'I think we may be related.'

The proffered hand was refused. 'Oh really? It must be of a somewhat obscure kinship I feel. I have no close relatives.'

'Was your husband Michael and your father Albert Rowlinson, who married Florence Parker?'

'Perhaps you should come in.' Mrs Mason led the way to a rather cluttered sitting room at the back of the terraced house. Angela caught a glimpse of the "best" room, with its uncomfortable Victorian furniture. A strange smell hung over the house, a compound of lavender furniture polish and mothballs. The latter may have emanated from Jean's dress, which would have been new when King George V celebrated his Jubilee.

'Would you like some tea?'

Angela accepted the offer with thanks and looked around. The old fashioned range was still in place, but her hostess filled a small electric kettle.

Jean caught her visitor looking at the range. 'I never light that now. It's far too much trouble. I have gone all electric!' She spoke quite gaily. 'Of course, when we moved here... but, before I tell you any secrets of my life, perhaps you will kindly explain how you believe us to be related.'

Angela took a deep breath. All that she had found out was in the public domain. Once the 1871 census had become available she had, like Edward, trawled through it to find her Simpson ancestors. She had been amazed to discover that in her great-grandparents' household in Melcester there was a child that none of them had known about. Lillie was, as far as they all knew, the eldest, followed by George, Maggie and finally her grandmother, Edith. But the census revealed that Great-Grandfather George, a "tea dealer" aged twenty-seven, also had a son, Albert, who was four years old. But for four years now, this had been accessible to anyone who chose to spend long hours in the county record office. She had painstakingly trawled through records to find Albert and his descendants and she was almost certain that Jean was his daughter.

'I believe that your father and my grandmother were brother and sister.'

'Indeed? And what was her name? Your grandmother, that is.'

'Edith Walker, née Simpson.'

'If her maiden name were Simpson, how is it that her brother had another name?'

Angela had to think quickly. Did Jean Mason know the full history of her own father? Illegitimacy was a great scandal in the nineteenth century and Jean had been born in that period. Indeed, she knew from her own childhood how it had still been viewed in the middle of the twentieth century. Albert was born in 1866; his mother, Margaret Rowlinson, had only married George the following year. 'I looked in the census for 1871. I found their household.' She fumbled in her handbag for the transcript she had made. 'Would you like to look at it?'

Jean rose. 'Let me pour that tea! And have a biscuit; they're quite fresh I think.' She proffered a tin which had been produced for the 1937 coronation. Angela noticed the monogram: *E VIII R*. 'Yes, the king who gave it all up. Perhaps that is appropriate!'

She sat down and took the A4 sheet covered with Angela's neat italic script. 'Would you pass me my glasses please? They are on the sideboard.' She read aloud the first part.

'"8, Clarence Villas, George Simpson, Head of House, grocer 27." Is that his age?' Angela nodded. 'Oh, I see, then "Margaret, Wife, Albert, son aged 4, Lillie, daughter aged 3 and George, son aged 1".' She laid the sheet of paper down. 'So, all this was collected in the census just over a hundred years ago? Where is your grandmother, Edith, did you say her name was?'

'She wasn't born until 1875. This is 1871,' Angela explained.

'Oh, I see.' She nodded. 'So why has it only just come to your attention?'

'It's the one hundred year rule. The detailed information collected in the census must not be disclosed until after a century has elapsed.'

'I see!' Jean passed the paper back. 'So, I'm still a bit confused, where do you fit in?'

'George and Margaret had two more children, Maggie, or Margaret, and Edith. Edith was my grandmother.'

'But my father's name was Rowlinson.' She seemed quite impassive. 'Your Albert is, evidently, Simpson.'

'George the grocer and Margaret his wife are my great-grandparents. I wanted to know what sort of lifestyle they had, so when the 1871 census became available, I went to the county record office in Melcester and did a search. This…' she waved the paper, 'is the result.'

The only response was a sound which might have been described as a grunt.

'But then I looked for the marriage record and found that they were married in September 1867. I have the marriage certificate, a copy… but Albert had been born to Margaret over a year earlier. So, he was illegitimate.' Angela didn't know how to continue.

There was a long pause. 'I suppose it is many years ago.'
Angela waited.

'May I ask how, given the difference in name, you were able to work out our relationship?' Angela was relieved that Jean seemed to have accepted that she was genuine.

'If you know someone's approximate date and place of birth, you can get a birth certificate. So I found out that your grandparents were not married and that the birth was registered in your grandmother's name, Rowlinson. There was no father given on the birth certificate.' She paused, hoping that Jean would disclose the paternity.

After a long pause Jean spoke again. 'My supposed grandfather was a good man.' Angela nodded. 'He married my grandmother, even though she had,' there was a pause, 'a bastard child. He provided well for her, but then died young, of consumption.' Angela's nod was more vigorous this time; she had George's death certificate. 'She herself died about the time I was born. She was grateful to him. Let me show you something.' She rose and disappeared into the front room, returning a few seconds later with a Bible. 'Read that!'

It was open at the fly leaf and Angela read aloud a handwritten inscription.

'"Margaret Simpson, from her affectionate husband George Simpson 1877. Arise, shine, for thy light is come".'

'It was given to my grandmother, as you see, by her husband. He was dying of consumption. Now that does not sound as though he were a wicked seducer!' There was a mixture of triumph, defiance and even maliciousness in her tone.

'I know he died in 1877; I have his death certificate...'

'But you want to know who the father of my father was.'

'Well…' It was one of the reasons that Angela had sought out her… first cousin once removed, as Jean must be. She nodded.

Jean took a deep breath. 'It was a long time before I knew that there was anything odd about my family. We were quite happy, three girls—'

'They aren't alive now, of course?' Angela in fact had already traced them.

'No. Dorothy died in 1950, Constance died in 1946. I've been here alone since then.'

'It was the family home, I believe?'

'Yes. Father brought Mother here just before Dorothy was born… we were all born here, our parents died here and my sisters died here.' She paused. The obvious comment that Jean herself would also die here was not made. Angela waited. Jean continued. 'But how did you know that?'

'The birth certificates of you and your sisters are—'

'Of course. Dorothy and Constance never left home; they were, respectively, a dressmaker and a teacher in an elementary school, as we called them in those days. I moved to a new house in the autumn of 1914, when I married Michael. Did you find that marriage also?' Angela nodded. 'Then he volunteered and was killed in one of the first engagements of that…' She paused. 'I use the word in both senses, bloody business. I was pregnant at the time of Michael's death; he never saw his son. We named him after his grandfather, who was still alive then of course. But then,' her voice trembled a little, 'our son, Albert, was killed at Dunkirk. I became a pacifist. I joined the Society of Friends, much to the disgust of my sisters who were devout C of E.' She paused and added by way of explanation, 'Quakers, you know.'

Angela did know. Quakers were the only religious group with whom she could feel any sympathy. She felt helpless in the face of this tragedy. Jean did not seem to seek pity, and although her instinct was to put her arms around her and hug her, she felt such a gesture would not be welcomed.

'I came back here, with the baby, and kept house for my parents and sisters. Two Alberts!' She smiled. 'My father was not the easiest of men, likely to fly off the handle at the slightest thing and he rather tended to bear grudges. My son had a sunny nature, but he was spoilt, by four women, as indeed was his grandfather.' Jean fell silent.

Angela was impatient to know the paternity of the elder Albert, and it was only by a supreme effort that she avoided prompting her hostess in some way. Brightly, and half rising as she spoke, she asked, 'Shall I make us another cup of tea?'

Jean seemed offended. 'I am not ready for more and I was always brought up to believe that the host or hostess should offer, not that the guest should demand.' She stressed the last word slightly.

'I'm sorry; I didn't mean to be rude…'

'But you are impatient for me to continue.' Mrs Mason permitted herself a ghost of a smile. 'And,' she glanced at the long case clock that stood in the corner, 'it is nearly lunchtime. But I'm going to allow you to have the run of my kitchen and I shall just sit here whilst you make some more tea, and, as it's getting near lunchtime, perhaps a spot of something else to eat.'

Angela was delighted to be able to be busy. 'What have you got in your store cupboards, Jean? I may call you that?'

Her cousin nodded. 'We always use Christian names in Quakers. I'm afraid… Angela, isn't it? I have very little in. There are some eggs…'

'Shall I do us some scrambled eggs then?'

'That would be lovely. I wish I had some bacon. I never buy it; it doesn't seem worthwhile for just me.'

'Would the corner shop have some?'

'I expect so. Though they're Muslims, would they be allowed to? Such nice young men, always so cheery. You could try. Here, take my key, then I don't have to bounce up to answer the door.'

Jean suddenly seemed more relaxed and older, too, Angela noted. The corner shop did indeed stock bacon. She bought some; it was grilled; bread was toasted and eggs were scrambled. Tea was made. She was relieved that she did not have to use the range. Marmalade was produced. 'My own make,' Jean proudly stated.

As they sat over a third cup of tea, Angela returned to the paternity of Jean's father.

'My father grew up in happy ignorance of his parentage, and in the assumption that he was born in wedlock to George Simpson and Margaret, née Rowlinson, his wife. My grandmother and her children and all the others lived in the family home. George, my grandfather, was dead by then of course.'

'That was in Morecambe?' Angela asked.

'Yes; after my grandfather died, my grandmother wanted a break. They had careers that forced them to go their separate ways. Albert had initially been apprenticed to a bookseller in Morecambe, but he had a row with him, I suppose, and decided to join the Lancashire police. When he first applied to join, he had to produce a birth certificate. And the dreadful truth, as it was of course seen in those days, was revealed. It didn't preclude his entering the police. But there was a row of some sort. One of his half-siblings taunted him as being a bastard. I think that word was used. The rest of the family returned to Melcester. He was given various police appointments, latterly here in Brungerley, but then he left the police and became a school attendance officer.'

'Children can be very cruel!'

There was an agonising pause which Angela longed to fill with some action or speech. At length, Jean continued. 'I only know this from Dorothy; he confided in her and made her vow not to speak of it again until after both he and Mother were dead. Somewhere just before the time of his marriage, I suspect, his temper flared up and he moved out from the parental home and never returned, though at least he kept up with his mother, Margaret, my grandmother, until she died. Then all contact with them was lost, it seems. Until today, that has been the case.' She smiled. 'I think I'm glad you came, my dear. Neither of us caused it; those who did are long dead, but the breach is healed. We never knew who Albert's father was. And we can't ever find out now! If George were the father, he waited a long time. It was over a year after the boy's birth before he married the mother.'

'It would be more likely that he would marry her before the birth of the child,' Angela suggested.

'Unless he had to wait until his apprenticeship was

over. I suspect that apprentices were not allowed to marry until that was the case.'

'I had wondered if it could be. His twenty-first birthday was exactly one month after Albert's birth.' Angela showed Jean some more of her transcriptions. 'But the rule about apprentices not marrying was ended earlier in the century.'

Jean studied them. 'You've done a lot of work on this, my dear. I think we can forgive our ancestress. A young girl's foolishness. And it means that George, who is your ancestor, though not mine, was a good and noble man, who, like Joseph, feared not to take unto him Margaret as his wife.' Angela smiled to show her understanding of the scriptural allusion. 'Though, given the rows there seem to have been in the Simpson household, the Holy Spirit may not really have been all that much in evidence!' She smiled. 'What happened to the other half-siblings?' She peered at the sheets. 'Lillie, George, Maggie and Edith. Which one are you descended from, dear?'

'Edith was my grandmother. She married Frederick Walker. But that's another story. As for the others, I can't find them anywhere; they seem to have disappeared. I found you by trailing through to find the marriage of an Albert Rowlinson, after I learned that he had been so registered. It was quite a long shot really and it was only after I'd spent ages trying to find a marriage of Albert Simpson.' She laughed. 'Then I found his children, and your marriage. County record office staff got to know me very well!'

'Edith?' Jean seemed to spend a moment or two in thought. 'I believe Dorothy, my eldest sister, you know, said that Father did have some contact with her until… oh dear!'

Angela raised her eyebrows quizzically.

'Her husband forbade it; that must be your grandfather.' Jean paused, embarrassed.

'I gather that he was a very difficult man. I'm not offended. I never really knew him; he died in the year I was born.'

'But you have the marriage certificate; what does that tell us about Albert's own father? Who was my grandfather?' Jean seemed as excited as a child as she suddenly realised the possibility of discovering her origin.

'Nothing. There's just a line drawn through the places where "father's name" and "father's occupation" are to be written. Your mother's name was Florence, wasn't it, Jean?' Angela fumbled in her bag.

'Florence, Florence Parker. Why do you ask? You already knew that.'

'A and F! Of course! I think it makes sense of a few bits of letters I've got. I'll bring them with me next time I come. I thought I had them with me.'

Shortly afterwards Angela made her farewells and left, promising to return and show Jean the letters. But it was not to be. Her letter enquiring when would be a suitable date was returned from a solicitor's office informing Angela that "… Mrs Mason has passed away…".

Chapter 4

1991

'Oh yes,' Mollie remembered. 'The scandalous Bertie.'

'Albert. We don't know if he was known as Bertie. Hang on!' Edward went into the small room they grandly styled the "study", pulled open a drawer and brought out a huge scroll of the Simpson family tree as far as he had been able to draw it up. 'Maggie was assumed to be the last survivor of the children of George, yes, I remembered his name correctly, his father was also George. Of course it's that silly ditty Charlie likes to chant, "Charlie, Freddie, Jimmy, George—" Anyway, the younger George married Margaret Rowlinson.'

'So?'

'Well, when Maggie Powell died intestate, the money had to go back to common ancestors. See…' He pointed to the relevant part. 'That was Samuel Rowlinson on Margaret's side, fifty per cent and George Senior, fifty per cent.'

'But they were dead, long before that!' protested Mollie.

'Yes, but then you come down, to the next generation. Samuel only had one other child, Arthur, whose daughter, Josephine, or Mrs Oliphant,' he pointed to the relevant part of the family tree, 'inherited the half. She probably only outlived Maggie by a few years and I've no idea what became of her money, or even if she had children to pass it on to.'

'She may have left it to a cats' home!'

Edward laughed. 'By the time Maggie died, all the cousins of her generation, including my grandfather, were dead, and so it came down to the next generation.'

'And that was your father…'

'Who spent most of it, and Charlie. They got a quarter each; quite a tidy sum, I forget how much.'

'But how do you know that any other Rowlinson is your relative?'

'Simpson is a common enough name, but Rowlinson isn't. And the association—'

'Who could it be?' Mollie looked hard at the diagram.

'I assumed Albert had died. He wasn't mentioned on the original genealogical table drawn up for probate, look! But he was really a Rowlinson, not a Simpson.'

'But if he were still alive in 1951, why was there no mention of him?'

'Family rows? Or he just moved away somewhere and lost touch.'

'It seems unlikely; wouldn't the solicitors have tracked him down?'

'I don't know what happens in these cases.'

Mollie thought for a moment or two. 'When Great Aunt Alice died, she had left about a hundred pounds to a neighbour who had looked after her.'

'I remember.'

'And poor old Maurice Stones, the junior solicitor at

Royd and Thorne, had to spend ages trying to find her, the neighbour that is. She'd moved away.'

'But she was specifically mentioned as a legatee,' Edward pointed out. 'Maggie Powell died intestate.'

'Why are you worried?' Mollie asked her husband.

'Because if Albert lived and had children, they might have a claim on the estate.'

'But it's forty years ago! Surely there must be a statute of limitations or something.'

'I could ask a solicitor.' Edward spoke rather dubiously. Suddenly he changed. With an almost conspiratorial air, he said, 'I know. I'll pretend that I'm writing a novel, draw up a family tree, more or less like this,' he waved the scroll at Mollie, 'and show it to… why don't we ask Maurice Stones?'

'He's a partner now, I believe. You could talk about drawing up wills. We ought to do that anyway.'

'Well, I could just drop it in as an afterthought. Ask him what happens in such cases.'

'Why don't you just describe the situation as it is?'

'Because if he did discover the truth, and the proceeds have to be redivided, he might feel duty-bound to report it and Charlie would lose *Wuthering Heights*. And I'd imagine that we would have to pay over the sum that my father inherited. I expect that when Charlie dies, most of it will come to us as he and Clara had no offspring… we must secure our future and that of our children. We could lose a lot initially and not gain anything when *Wuthering Heights* is sold. We must try to keep all this from that lot in Melcester somehow.'

Mollie sighed. After nearly twenty years of marriage she knew that Edward loved to create a cloak-and-dagger situation out of anything that others would regard as being quite straightforward.

*

Angela's curiosity had been aroused and a few days later, Edward received a letter. After a few brief pleasantries she came straight to the point:

> *... so I asked Henry if he knew his three times great-grandfather's name – I wouldn't have been in the least surprised if he hadn't; children seldom have any real interest in their ancestry, but apparently his great-uncle (Charles, isn't it?) had gone right back with the names of the male line and did a sort of chant with Henry when he was a kid – 'Charlie, Freddie, Jimmy, George'. Indeed, he showed him – Charles showed Henry that is – a family tree, though he – Charles that is – said you had a copy. Have you? Anyway, my twice great-grandfather is also a George Simpson. I think that will be the same generation as your George? He was born in 1810.*

Edward worried over this for several days. George Simpson, born in 1810, was indeed his great-great-grandfather. It seemed probable, or even certain, that Angela was of the same family as himself. He resolved to say nothing to Henry. He sent a non-committal letter to Angela:

> *... it seems unlikely. I personally have very little information on the family. My father died a few years ago, but in any case, Charlie, as the elder son, holds all the documents about*

the Simpson family. He lost his wife a few years ago and is now quite senile; I do not want to distress him unduly and therefore, at this stage, I do not want to investigate further.

This was quite untrue. Charlie had passed everything onto him and, although frail and dependent on the ministrations of his housekeeper, he was quite compos mentis. A sudden thought caused Edward to pause before sealing the letter and to consult something. He then added a postscript.

Like you I am amazed that Henry should show such an interest. I wonder if you have memorised the names of your own immediate ancestors. I would suppose that you would remember the names of your female ancestors? Was there someone with a Christian name beginning with E?

After he had posted the letter he regretted the P.S. What had prompted it was some letters Charlie had passed on. The name Walker – was it Frederick? He'd need to check, but it featured there and they were signed, somewhat enigmatically "E". Was Frederick Walker Angela's ancestor? Angela would probably write. He also wrote a letter to the housekeeper:

… seems possible that this cousin, Angela Walker, may try to gain access to my uncle. I do not want him distressed by such an invasion of his privacy and the probing questions that may be put to him. On no account are you let her into Wuthering Heights.

Angela replied almost by return:

... I loved the chant Henry told me, but although there's nothing like that in our family, I can tell you the outline. My father was Frank Walker who married Olwen Jones, who came from a little village in Wales. Frank's father, my grandfather, was Frederick Walker who married Edith Simpson in 1896. Her parents were George and Margaret Simpson who married in Melcester in 1867, although...

Edward dropped the letter and put his head in his hands as Mollie came in.

'Whatever's the matter, Edward?'

'This is ghastly.' He pointed to the letter, which had now fallen on the floor. 'Read it.'

She read it quickly and reached the next section:

Her parents were George and Margaret Simpson who married in Melcester in 1867, although Margaret had given birth to an illegitimate child, Albert, a year earlier...

'I see,' Mollie said, before continuing.

... I met the last surviving descendant of Albert a few years ago, just months before she died. That line has come to a full stop.

'So then,' Mollie said, handing the letter back, 'no worries about the inheritance.'

'Yes, that line has ended,' Edward agreed, 'but listen: *I am descended from the youngest sibling, Edith, who was born in 1875.* So she was born a year after Maggie. But there was no mention of Edith in the probate settlement. So this "commune" as Henry described it will be entitled to half that which Dad and Charlie got.'

'You'd better see Maurice Stones tomorrow. This week, while it's half-term and you are free.'

'I am not sure. If I do go through the rigmarole of supposedly writing a novel, he might twig that it's a sort of smokescreen. You know, like the people who say, a friend of mine has… then describe some difficult situation they are in and…'

Mollie interrupted him. 'If he is acting for you he will do what you want. Make out that it is fiction, the plot of a novel that you are writing if you insist, but find out if this Angela and the rest of them have a claim.'

'I am not going to risk it. If the Walkers do have a claim it will cause all sorts of problems.'

'Listen, Edward,' his wife spoke to him as though he were a rather recalcitrant infant, 'it will all come out in the end. You may as well know the worst. And it may not be as bad as you fear. There must be a statute of limitations or something?'

★

'So what brings you to see me then, Edward?' Maurice Stones waved his hand towards the easy chair to the side of the desk in his large office over the bank on the main street of Oakhill, the suburb of Leverford where the Simpsons lived.

'I am trying to write a novel about a lost inheritance.'

'I see.'

'Well, you acted for Mollie when her Great Aunt Alice died. Do you remember?'

'I certainly do. Took me ages to find the former neighbour, what was her name... oh yes, Jane Smith. The surname being what it was made it not exactly easy! And the amount was very small, was it a hundred quid?'

'If Jane Smith had died and there were kids, Auntie Alice's money would be due to them?'

Maurice nodded.

'Now suppose there had been a row and one kid had been disowned. So he or she was left out, perhaps he or she had kids and—'

'Edward, no one is going to worry over £100.'

'But suppose it had been a lot more, a real fortune...'

Maurice looked hard at him. 'This is not fiction, is it?'

Edward took a deep breath and explained the whole situation.

Maurice drew a deep breath before replying. 'I'm afraid that there could be a claim by this lot in Melcester. Let me have a close look at that family tree you say you've got.'

'I haven't brought it with me.'

'Drop it off sometime... and let me see, how about your coming in on Friday, say ten o'clock. That's a slot I keep for emergencies.'

*

Edward, who had returned with the family tree later the first day, arrived well before ten on the Friday. He sat uncomfortably in the outer office, smiling nervously at the middle-aged lady who was... what was she? A secretary? Or an office manager?

'Ah, hello Edward,' Maurice emerged from his office, picked up some papers from the desk then returned to his other client. 'Be with you in a second,' he called over his shoulder.

Their conversation seemed interminable and Edward became more and more agitated. Eventually the door opened and a middle-aged lady with a rather supercilious air came out.

'OK, come in now,' called Maurice. 'Sorry to have kept you waiting.' He waved Edward to a chair and closed the door.

'I am afraid that the "commune", as you term it, could claim. Edith was a full sibling of Maggie and so would have been entitled to a share. It would need a judge to give leave, but if they do not know… how much was the sum Maggie left?'

'I'm not sure exactly, but enough for Charlie to buy that place out towards Haworth.'

'Never mind, we can check that.'

'What do I do in the meantime?'

'I suggest you do nothing. Say nothing to anyone other than perhaps Mollie, but don't discuss it with your sons.'

Chapter 5

1996

Not much happened for a while and Edward's fears were eased. Henry and Joanna graduated and found jobs respectively in London and Birmingham. Henry visited Melcester several times; eventually, when Henry had telephoned Mollie, they arranged for Joanna to visit them in Leverford.

The following evening when Edward was at home the phone rang. 'Angela Walker here.' For a moment Edward could not think who this was. She spoke in rather an authoritative manner. 'I'm going to be in Leverford the day after tomorrow, Saturday, to see that exhibition at the City Art Gallery and hoped we might meet. I'd love to see if we are related and it's so much easier to chat face to face. I haven't been able to do much on family history lately with one thing and another.'

Edward could not imagine that there was a major exhibition. The art gallery was a typical small Victorian place with a few notable paintings and a lot of very run-of-the-mill stuff. 'What is it about?' he asked.

'Have you not seen it advertised? One of your city's favourite sons. Harold Dunwell. They are doing a retrospective of him.'

'I've never heard of him, I'm afraid.'

'He was born in Leverford!' She sounded almost accusatory, as though he were failing in not knowing about him; he was surely rather obscure.

Edward tried to cover his ignorance. 'I did see something in the *Express and Advertiser*, the local rag, you know. He was a painter in watercolours wasn't he?'

'Yes, mainly landscapes of the area. Some of them are rather effective, with the smoke and grime of your part of the world. Almost Turneresque.'

'I suppose so.' He was desperately trying to think of an excuse not to meet her, but, as he later put it to Mollie, he might as well get it over and done with; it was like a visit to the dentist. 'Err, what do you suggest? We could give you lunch here and—'

'Why don't we meet in the coffee bar of the gallery? I presume there is one?'

'Yes, there is.' Sometimes he had said that this was the only good thing about the gallery, with its ponderous staircases, marble busts and over ornately framed paintings; it seemed that the curators had tried to compensate for the mediocrity of the works by an elaborate packaging.

'My train gets in at 10.42. I see that the gallery is a couple of minutes' walk from the station.'

'Shall I meet you at the station?'

'No, I'll walk to the gallery. I'll be wearing a red anorak-type thing. I look forward to it!'

'Oh right…' but she had gone. He replaced the receiver and sat by the phone, his head in his hands.

'What on earth's the matter?' It was Mollie who had returned rather later from work than had her husband.

He explained the situation.

'Well, it will sort things out one way or another. Now, have you made dinner? It's getting late and you've got a church meeting haven't you?'

★

He found Angela sitting at a table eating a croissant and drinking coffee. She was indeed wearing a red anorak, a rather startling shade he felt for a sixty-year-old woman.

She waved her croissant at him. 'I love these; it makes me feel I am in France again. Perhaps, as it's morning, I should have had café au lait in a bowl, but Yorkshire doesn't run to such extravagancies, and anyway I do like it black. What can I get you?' She rose, picking up her handbag.

Edward's nice sense of propriety made him feel uneasy. A gentleman should buy the lady her food and drink, but it would be rude to refuse her offer.

'No, I'll…' But she was already on her way to the counter. 'I'll have the same please,' he asked weakly, sinking onto the chair.

For a while they chatted about croissants, coffee and France, discovering a mutual love of that country. Then she produced from her briefcase a folder with various scribblings and a family tree. She spread the latter on the table.[2] 'This is only a rough draft, but this is where we are… that's me, and there is Joanna.'

'Do you think that she and Henry will settle down together? Even get married? I'd love to have some grandchildren.'

---

[2] See the family tree on page 171.

'That's up to them, but they have been together for quite a while. Of course they are cousins, but pretty well removed so it isn't really dangerous their having kids together, if that is what they want.' She stressed the last word quite firmly.

'Of course.' He pored over the paper. 'Some of this is what I have known for a long time, ever since Maggie's death and the tree that was drawn up for probate. You hadn't found her marriage to Edmund Powell?'

'No. I know that my grandmother had siblings, Maggie and the other two, Lillie and George, but there seems to have been no contact and I knew nothing about what happened to them. I only latterly discovered the half-sibling, Albert, just before the death of the only surviving descendant, Jean Mason.'

'I remember, you told me in a letter about five years ago.' He tried to remember Angela's grandmother's name. She'd told him in a letter about five years ago and he had seen it on the family tree she had drawn up.

'So, Maggie married another Edward? When was that?' Her pen was poised over a notepad.

'No, Edmund. Edmund Powell, quite a wealthy industrialist.' As he said this he could have kicked himself.

'So she died a wealthy woman? Or did he go first? Did they have kids?'

'No they had no children. They married in 1936, so she was past child bearing.' He spoke shortly.

'So who did it all go to?'

He shuffled his feet. 'Err, would you like another coffee? Or is it time to be thinking about lunch?'

Angela laughed. 'I want to have a first look at the

exhibition before lunch and I daren't have a coffee now. Causes havoc with my ageing body if I have too much. So where did all the loot go?'

'On the Simpson side,' he explained hastily, 'it all went to the various cousins. Half went to the Rowlinsons. I forget the details.'

'Cousins? So we should have had a share of Maggie's loot? But it will be too late now anyway.'

He hung his head and shuffled his feet again, unwilling to lie.

'You mean we may be able to sue you for it?' She chuckled.

'Well, our solicitor, Maurice Stones, said it could be. Of course there would have to be a new investigation and—' He paused. 'But, you see it's not just the fact that Mollie and I would have to dig deeply, it's Uncle Charlie; he's very frail and living in *Wuthering Heights*, and—'

'*Wuthering Heights*?'

'When he came into the Powell money, he and his late wife Clara bought a rather nice detached house on the edge of the moors.' He waved his hand in the approximate direction. 'And they decided to give it that name. It's quite an ordinary stone-built detached house of the 1930s, pebble-dashed, mock Tudor gables, you know the sort of place.'

Angela nodded.

Edward continued, 'He has some money, but he would have to sell the place and—'

'Were they admirers of Emily Brontë's novel?'

'What? Oh I doubt if they had really studied the work, it was just the name and… but what are you going to do?'

'Do about what?'

'Claiming your inheritance.'

'I have no moral rights there. In 1951, Jean Mason, Albert's last surviving descendant, might have found it useful and I suppose my parents were also entitled to some, though they didn't need it. But it's ridiculous to suggest we have rights.'

'Actually, I don't think Albert's family were entitled to any, with his being only a half sibling and—'

'How ridiculous! Who said the law is an ass?'

'I don't know. But, you will let it be... as it is?'

'Of course. We don't need the money and in any case all this about legal rights to property is nonsense!'

Edward recalled that the *Fairholme* household were socialist.

'But the whole business is quite fascinating,' Angela continued. 'How and why did the family become split up?'

'Well, to begin at the beginning...'

'It is spring, moonless night in the small town...'

Edward laughed. 'You like *Under Milk Wood* too?'

'I love it; it somehow seems to break the pomposity of a small town.'

The ice had been broken and they began to piece together the story. But, although Angela had quite a few papers, Edward had brought nothing. 'Look,' he said, 'why don't you come back to our house? Mollie would love to meet you I'm sure, and then we can sort this out better when we look at the stuff I've accumulated.'

'I want to see the Dunwell exhibition first. And I have a ticket for the 16.26 train. How far out are you?'

'It's about half an hour on the bus. I seldom drive into the city centre.'

Angela did a rapid calculation. 'I'll spend about an hour here, grab some lunch, that would be about two o'clock, then out to your house for 2.30… is it worth it as I'd need to leave at about half three to be sure of catching the train? Let's meet again and give it a whole day. You could come to Melcester, both of you, and stay overnight.'

'Or you stay with us? We have a couple of spare rooms now that the boys have left. At least while James is at university.'

They pulled out their diaries and made provisional arrangements for a weekend the following month. Edward left the art gallery feeling very relieved, but on the bus his anxieties returned. Angela had waived her claim; would her siblings, Mary and William, be as generous?

★

On his return to the house he realised that the date that he and Angela had chosen coincided with Joanna's first visit to Leverford. Both bedrooms would be needed. He rang his elder son to tell him about the clash of dates.

'You and Joanna can share your room because Angela, her aunt, is coming that same weekend. We are going to compare notes on family ancestry.'

It was Henry who was embarrassed. 'I thought, Dad, that you and Mum would'

'Would what? Disapprove? It's 1996, not 1896! In any case, we need James's room for Angela.'

'Well, I could sleep downstairs, on the sofa?'

'And go tiptoeing upstairs at dead of night for a lovers' tryst? No, let's be sensible.'

'But why on earth is Angela coming, Dad?'

'Well you know we are related?'

'I thought you were shying away from that for some reason?'

'I had been. When Maggie Powell died and we inherited some of her wealth, as did Charlie and some of Maggie's mother's family, all seemed fine. But now it appears that Angela and Joanna and the others might have a claim, as they were not found and put on the tree drawn up for probate.'

'Tree?'

'Family tree…'

'Oh don't try to explain, I can't take it in. Fax it to me at work.'

Henry rang next morning. 'I've pored over that tree, but where are Joanna and the others?'

His father explained. 'That is basically what was drawn up for Maggie's will… but she had two other siblings. The elder was called Albert. I've pencilled him on, perhaps that hasn't copied well, but I haven't got his descendants yet. Angela has found them, or at least where they were. None now survives.'

'So where do Jo and her lot come from?'

'There was another sibling, Edith, born in 1875; she is their ancestor. She was first cousin to Frederick, your great-grandfather.'

'So Jo and I are cousins?'

'Fourth cousins.'

'Err, should we… I mean…'

'It's only first cousins where there are problems, I think. But are you thinking of marrying and having kids?'

'No, yes, I dunno. But should Jo's lot have had a share of Maggie's loot then?'

'If they put in a claim, possibly, but Angela assures me that they don't want to pursue it.'

'I suppose that is a relief to you.'

'And even more for Uncle Charlie; at least it would be if he knew anything about this.'

*

But Edward decided it was now time to sound out Charlie. He visited *Wuthering Heights* quite frequently but so far had said nothing to his uncle about the cousins he had discovered. He decided to take the bus as it dropped him on the main road right outside the house. He let himself in with his own key and called out, 'Hello Charlie! Are you at home or are you out jogging, or chasing the girls?' Both of these were standing jokes. The first was because after a short stay in hospital following a minor operation, Edward asked him how he was and his uncle replied that he'd given up jogging. In fact he could only move with difficulty even before the stay in hospital. The other was because at the day centre he attended, whereas most of the people were not only frail physically but were in the early stages of dementia or similar complaints, Charlie was bright and cheerful and had been referred to as "my boyfriend" by one of the young care assistants, who put her arm round him as she said this.

'I'm in here, Edward.'

"Here" was the main lounge that ran the whole of the length of the south side of the house. Much of the external wall had windows that gave a view of the moors and lent some justification for the name that Charlie and Clara had given it. The furniture was of that curiously spindle-legged type popular in the 1950s when they moved in. He recalled that Clara had told him that she wanted everything to be new. Edward had no idea what had happened to their original furniture; he was too young at the time to have cared.

'Pull up another chair and bring that table up,' Charlie said. 'It's teatime at the zoo, but go into the kitchen and make sure that Grace knows you're here.' Edward moved off. 'And ask her if there is any more of that Victoria sponge cake.'

A few minutes later when they were sipping tea and enjoying the sponge cake Edward felt it not inappropriate to mention to his uncle about the discoveries of some long-lost cousins.

'Err, Charlie, I've found out some family history, going right back.' He paused, knowing what was coming.

'I can go back four generations and five if we include you, Charlie, Freddie, Jimmy, George.' He counted these on his fingers. 'Now that is a long way back. Have you gone back further?'

'Well, George who was born in 1810 had sons...'

'That would be Jimmy, James, my grandfather, I never knew him. He died quite young I think, but Grandma always shut up like... what is it that shuts up?'

'A clam?' Edward suggested.

'Yes... well she was like a clam about James, and he was her husband. I don't know what was wrong with him.'

This was news to Edward, but for the moment he thought it better to say nothing about it and return to the cousins. 'As well as James there was his brother George, a bit older, named after his father who was also George.'

'He was Maggie Powell's father I think… it's all on that family tree I drew up, isn't it? That was a palaver. All the sorting out but it was worth it in the end. Your auntie loved living here. She'd grown up in a back-to-back in Shedford. There were six of them crammed into a little place and it was damp and there were rats…'

Edward had heard most of it before, many times. Curiously, it had never been Clara, Charlie's wife, who had described the living conditions in Shedford. He supposed that in some way Charlie had believed he had saved her. Even before their windfall from the late Maggie he had sufficient income to buy a nice little semi in a similar location to where Edward and his family lived.

'… so you see her life had been hard. It's such a pity that she didn't live longer to enjoy it all.'

'Yes, well, it seems that Maggie had some siblings.'

'Maggie Powell?'

'Yes.'

'Now if I remember rightly there was Auntie Lillie, she was a dressmaker and Uncle George, he was a chemist and helped run the family business with my father, but Father died young and George decided to pull out. Neither of them married and they died before the war. I can't remember the dates but I remember their funerals. It was sad because we often went round for tea, well to Lillie's, and George would sometimes be there. She baked lovely cakes and he was great fun. He had another name as well as George.'

'Yes, I know; it was Clarence. But I've found a couple of others of the family.'

'Which family?'

'Lillie, George and Maggie had an older brother, Albert and a younger sister, Edith.'

'How can you know that? We never knew anyone of that name.'

Edward described his search, Henry's meeting Joanna and his own meeting with Angela.

'So all these are cousins?'

Edward nodded.

'I can't take it all in. It might be nice to meet them sometime though.'

Edward decided not even to hint at the possibility of a claim on the inheritance. It might never happen; indeed Angela said they would not pursue any claim, but at least Charlie was in some way prepared.

'I got Ahmed to drive me up into the Dales again last week.' Ahmed, a cheerful young man whose family came from the Punjab, had been engaged by Charlie as a part-time chauffeur. 'You know my grandmother, who of course is your great-grandma, Patience? She was Miss Vaughan before she married; well, she came from a farm in Wharfedale.'

Edward did know and also knew how Patience took the family out to the farm on Saturdays in summer. He knew the exact time of train they caught from Leverford's Fraser Square station, the time of the return and the usual food they had at teatime. But he also knew he had to listen to it again as he had so many times before. He allowed his mind to wander until he heard Charlie say something he had never mentioned before.

'But one of the aunties – was it Emily or was it Eleanor? – said something about a long-lost cousin. Was she called

Edith? They had met somewhere but as she was telling me, Grandma appeared and her look told Auntie to shut up.'

This was intriguing; Edward recalled his earlier comment, Patience shutting up like a clam about her husband. Perhaps this was also to do with his great-grandfather, James. In one of the letters he had there was an E and now, as well as his great-aunts, Emily and Eleanor, there was another E. In Angela's letter about six years ago, she had told him her grandmother's name and he had seen it on the family tree she had showed him the previous day. Was she "Edith"?

Charlie had launched into one of his oft-repeated tales about catching a train to Ilkley and how he and Edward's father, who was not much more than a toddler at the time, had climbed up to the Cow and Calf rocks and disappeared round the back of these crags creating a minor panic among the older ones. 'They were looking for us everywhere and saying they'd have to tell the police and then we appeared on the top of the Cow, or was it the Calf? Oh there was such a to-do... but it was that day that Auntie... whichever one it was... told me something about the long-lost cousin. It would be nice if we could meet her.' He paused. 'Should she have had a share in Maggie Powell's money?'

Edward groaned inwardly; it would have been better if he had not started this conversation. 'Oh no!' he said brightly. 'It's too late for them to claim now.'

This seemed to satisfy his uncle.

Edward stood up. 'Actually, I do need to be getting back. I need to get some things sorted out for next half-term.' This was not entirely untrue, but his real reason was to avoid any probing questions by Charlie.

As he walked down the drive to catch the bus he looked back at the house. As he knew, since Charlie and Clara bought this place, house prices had gone up considerably more than other things. No one would get permission to build here now and that would add something to the value. The design was unimaginative; it was almost a cube built from the local sandstone but with little half-timbered gables stuck on above the first-floor windows. Inside, the rooms were small and the layout was such that there was a lot of wasted space, but the outlook was magnificent; it could be extended. If Charlie were forced to sell to repay the inheritance then there would be plenty left over so that he would be able to live comfortably for the rest of his life and as he was now ninety-two, that might not be long. In fact, perhaps things could be held up until after Charlie's death, allowing him to live out his days, and then they could sell the place and divide the proceedings; he assumed Charlie had left everything to him. But on the other hand if… so he worried until he reached home and Mollie calmed him down.

Chapter 6

1996

Angela arrived with a briefcase that seemed to have a great deal in it. 'I think these might be of interest,' she said, dumping the contents on the dining room table. Edward had suggested that it would be the best place to spread out the various sheets.

'So you found out what happened to Albert and where he was born?' Edward asked. 'I got that he was born in Charnborough, but didn't find how or what happened to him.

'He was born in the house of a Rowlinson cousin, and then informally adopted by George, who married his mother.'

'I got that, but what happened to him eventually?'

'Well, I remember that Grandma had said something about their living in Morecambe after her father died. She, my grandmother, was only two at the time. So I went to Lancashire County Record Office and found them in a trade directory; the 1881 census wasn't yet available. She, Margaret, my great-grandmother, was keeping a boarding house. Albert was there, and all the others including my grandmother, Edith.'

'I assumed he must have died. What was he doing? He'd have had some sort of trade or profession by then, wouldn't he?'

'Later, I discovered from Jean Mason, his daughter, that he was apprenticed to a bookseller. Then I found that in the 1881 census, when I was able to get to it.'

'Ah.'

'On a sudden hunch I wondered if he got married there or anything, so trawled through the St Catherine's House registers looking for Albert Simpson and found nothing, at least nothing of "our" Albert.'

'I tried that; there are a hell of a lot of Simpsons.'

'So I decided to look for him as Rowlinson. There was no formal adoption in those days, so his surname was that, not Simpson. He married Florence Parker in 1890. She was a barmaid! It was definitely our guy, right age and later on, when I could get the 1891 census, I saw he was born in Charnborough. Jean Mason, the one who I saw just before she died, told me quite a bit, but she didn't tell me that about her mother!' Angela laughed.

She showed Edward a bundle of letters. 'They were in a Bible that belonged to my grandmother.'

'I thought you were an atheist.' Edward smiled.

'I am, but I value history.'

'I have some letters too; I've got them here. Uncle Charlie passed them on to me. They were at the back of a drawer in a bureau and Charlie has no idea where they came from… he wonders if it was possibly from his father or "one of the aunts". They are signed "E".'

'Could that be Edith, my grandmother?'

'Well, they cannot be from either of his aunts. If you

read through these letters you will see that whoever sent them is not living in Yorkshire and the aunts, they were my great-aunts actually, Emily and Eleanor, never left Yorkshire.

'Ah, yes,' said Angela as she read through the first of them, 'this suggests the letter was from somewhere other than the county of the White Rose. "One always imagines that Yorkshire receives much worse weather than the rest of the country." But wait a minute, "8, C Villas", Clarence Villas, that was the family home of Margaret and George; they were there in 1871, then returned to the same house after some time in Morecambe.'

'Why did they go to Morecambe?'

'I'm guessing that Margaret wanted to get away from Melcester after George died.'

'Wait a minute,' interposed Edward, 'who are Margaret and George?'

Angela pointed to the family tree. 'My great-grandparents.'

'Ah,' said Edward, 'so that all makes sense with the writer of this letter being Edith, your grandmother. Who is this Dora that calls your grandmother, if it is indeed her, "Auntie E"?'

'It's got to be Dorothy, Albert and Florence's eldest, Jean Mason's sister.'

'I've got a postcard as well. It was sent to one of my great-aunts in the summer of 1936 from Keswick. Look at the stamp, Edward the Eighth; he reigned for most of that year.'

'Well, yes, but they only got the stamps out late in 1936, the year he came to the throne, then they had to last through to the next year, when his brother was king. Can you read the date?'

'It's blurred.'

'May I see?' Angela's hand was outstretched. Edward passed the card over. 'St Andrew's Terrace. Is that the Simpson family home?'

'Yes, Great-Aunts Emily and Eleanor lived there with Sarah, their widowed sister-in-law, my grandmother; I never knew the great-aunts as they died before I was born. The addressee might be either of them but I have no idea who the "E" that was sending it could be. And then there are other Es… not me of course… but look: "here with E and me. Fondest love E." Quite baffling.' Edward laughed.

Angela, scrabbling in her bag, was not listening. 'Ah, here it is!' She produced a very similar postcard. 'This was sent to me! Look! These link together.'

Edward took the card. 'Baby Angela? Err… so you were around then?'

'I was born in 1936 but only late in the year, the 5th of November, would you believe, and I was baffled as it is obviously a summer holiday, but I discovered that throughout 1937, at least certainly in the summer, they were using Edward the Eighth stamps. This date is blurred too, but the month is July. Daft sending a postcard to a babe, but they did that sort of thing in those days.'

'So who might have sent it?'

Angela dived into her bag and produced a family tree. 'It's really been sent to my mother, or "Mama".' She pointed to the tree. 'Olwen Walker, née Jones, by her mother or "Grandmama", see?' She pointed to the family tree. 'Edith Walker née Simpson. But also by "Cousin E".'

'Who must be one of my great-aunts!' exclaimed Edward.

'So, Edith kept some sort of contact with your Simpsons in Leverford.'

'I have something from a Bible.' Edward produced the flyleaf with the life events of the Simpsons of Melcester. 'This was with Maggie's things when she died and it was used to establish probate. Albert is not on it. After I discovered him in the 1871 census I assumed that it was because he had died, but I guess it's because he was illegitimate.'

'May I look?' She studied it for a while. 'I wonder who wrote it. It would be interesting to know.' She laughed. 'Get a graphologist on it. But that's odd… Lillie, George and Maggie are on it, but Edith, my grandmother, is not. And look,' she pointed, 'the bottom bit has been neatly cut off. Grandma has been cut off! Literally, because none of her sister's fortune came to her descendants.'

Edward looked worried. 'Err…'

'Don't worry; I've said we are not going to try to get it!' She patted his arm.

'And are your brother and sister in agreement with that… William and Mary?'

'Of course. "Property is theft"!'

'Was that Marx?' Edward's conservative feelings were in conflict with the relief he felt that there would be no claim.

Angela laughed. 'No, it's Proudhon, who predates Marx, but I don't think we should have a political discussion, not yet at least. I suggest we sit down and look at these letters first, carefully, and see if we can make anything of them.

See if they match at all.'

They began with Angela's letters. 'It is so annoyingly imprecise,' she complained. '"16, St A Terrace" and "Sunday afternoon".'

'Of course, that's St Andrew's Terrace, Leverford,' Edward put in. 'The family lived there from, well, probably from when they were built until Granny died in 1951. Quite a posh terraced house, narrow with four floors. Women-killers, my mother called them!'

'There is this fragment, a P.S. "… delighted that she has found A and his new wife…" That has to be Albert, I'd guess, as she goes on to say that this is in Lancashire, so it has to be just after 1890 when Albert and Florence got married. "G" must be his brother George, or rather his half-brother. There was a row when it was discovered that Albert was illegitimate.'

'Wait a minute!' interposed Edward. 'There's another, longer fragment here, "find a way to continue to write". So there was not just a row, but a real breach between Albert and his siblings?'

'Apparently, so Jean Mason told me. She also said that her father, Albert that is, had contact with Edith, my grandmother, until her husband forbade it.' Angela laughed. 'She told me that he was a difficult man and that ties in with other things I know about him.'

'So he would forbid contact between his wife, Edith, and her brother, or half-brother, Albert, because the latter was illegitimate?'

'It would seem so. And here is something that I have tried to work on. "… your Mr W", that must refer to my grandfather, Frederick Walker.'

'Wait a minute...' Edward fumbled through his own letters. 'The "affectionate cousin" as she describes herself is possibly going to marry Mr Walker, a "dissenter".'

'May I look?' She pored over the letter, then read aloud. '"I do love our church here and we are privileged to have had some of the customs of the Medieval Church restored. My brother is very disapproving, saying it is like Rome". I know they were Free Church, not Anglicans. I had thought it was because they were freethinkers and somehow foreshadowed my father's declaration, after the First World War, that he was an atheist, but this seems to suggest otherwise. "I fear he intends to make a Dissenter of me. Certainly our children would have to be brought up in the faith of their father". What trials women had to bear!'

'I did try to work out where that might be, an Anglo Catholic parish church and a Dissenting chapel, called Providence, on the other side of the town, but it was impossible.'

'No, if she'd given the dedication of the church it might have helped. The nearest church to Clarence Villas is St John's and it is quite "high", as I understand. But Providence Chapel I don't know. Edith and Frederick bought *Fairholme* at the time of their marriage in 1890; 8, Clarence Villas was the home of George and Margaret after their marriage.'

'Of course I knew that from the 1871 census,' interposed Edward.

'After George's death they all went to Morecambe, but it seems that Margaret and the children, George was dead of course, returned to 8, Clarence Villas after Albert married Florence in 1890.'

'Where did they get married?'

'Albert and Florence? In Morecambe, "According to the Rites and Ceremonies of the Established Church", as the marriage certificate states.'

'A wise choice, perhaps, to marry in Morecambe. Sorry, that was a feeble joke.'

Angela chuckled. 'Perhaps this is getting too serious. But my grandparents didn't get married in Providence, wherever that might have been, but in the huge town centre place that was the main URC church until they finally got permission to demolish it a few years back. It was a Congregational church.'

'There are quite few of that sort in the West Riding too; or rather there were. Like yours, many have been demolished. I always think of their being the sort of place where the couples in *When We Are Married* were involved.'

'That is a good play; there are some almost feminist touches.'

'Feminist!' exclaimed Edward.

'One of the women tells her pompous husband that he is dull, dreary and stingy and that she's had enough!'

Edward laughed. 'I suppose so!'

'It is stretching it a bit,' Angela admitted. 'But to business. I found George, my great-grandfather, and his brother, James, your great-grandfather, in the earlier censuses but by 1871 James has disappeared. I now assume that he went to Leverford?'

Edward nodded. 'In early 1871 he is there, in the census, and he marries Patience Vaughan later that year. By the 1881 census they are in St Andrew's Terrace.'

'What brought him to Leverford?'

'He had evidently trained as a pharmacist, apprenticed to someone in Melcester, I assume, and then bought a business here.'

'Now, as I can see here,' Angela pointed to the family tree Edward had drawn up, 'he had three children.'

'Two girls and my grandfather, Frederick.'

'You have the women's dates of death. What happened to James? Do you know when he died?'

'James just disappears; I cannot find any record of his death, which is odd. George Clarence takes over running the business, it seems, as Frederick is only just twenty-one and Emily obviously couldn't.'

'No, of course, women can't do things like that. They are poor, weak-minded creatures.'

'I'm sorry, Angela, but that is how it was in the Victorian era.'

'I know, I know. But have you not tried to search for him?'

'Have you any idea how many James Simpsons born in 1849 there are?'

'A lot, I know. I've tried to find him too, but I thought as you know more about him, you'd get further.'

They pored over the various pieces of evidence for a while and then began to draw up a plan. Angela took charge. 'If we focus on this, one of those sent to Leverford, to whichever of your great-aunts. Listen: "He says that your family is, tainted".'

'Wait a minute.' Edward took back the letter. 'I suggest we study all these letters silently and see what we can make of them, then come back and piece things together. You stay in here; I'll go to what we laughingly call "The Study". We'll need to swap the letters about.'

★

'Well,' Edward said after half an hour or so, 'what do you make of it all?'

'Initially, all seems well. Your great-aunt, who is a dressmaker—'

'Hang on,' said Edward, 'I know that from my earlier research. Emily, the elder, was the dressmaker. Here…' He pointed to the family tree.

'So she was three years older than Edith, my grandmother, near enough contemporaries.'

'Somewhere in the spring of this year a dreadful discovery was made, which, added to the illegitimacy of Albert, caused a rift. And I am fairly sure that the year is 1895.'

'How?'

'She writes, "… the worst winter that she has known in all her fifty-odd years…" and she was born in 1843. Plus…' he paused dramatically, 'I know from my climatology that 1895 was a bad winter.'

'But what to make of this, I don't know,' Angela said, '"Let us hope that his removal… he shouted the words… Your Abominable Brother-in-Law" from Edith ties in with Emily's "I cannot really bring myself to tell you what I only dimly understand myself, but it seems that events in London reported in the *Telegraph*," which we take, have had their echo here. It was Mama's reading these reports that made her realise what Papa was.'

'The "brother-in-law" or "Papa" are James, my great-grandfather. What can he have been up to? It seems as though A and F and their children must be Albert and Florence and the children including therefore the Jean

Mason you met. They seem to have been the go-betweens for a meeting between… who?'

'That is an intriguing bit as it is only a fragment.' Angela read, "'… and Calf. It was fortunate that we did not go the following day for a great flood occurred in the town and I doubt we would have been able to catch a train home. All my planning and scheming to be finally able to see him after five years would have come to naught. He brought his friend. I had always thought he was a nice person". So Emily is writing this to Edith, my grandmother; who is he and who is his friend? There is more, but if we knew what the Calf was… it's a capital letter so it is not a farm animal…'

'Wait a minute!' Edward spoke excitedly. 'That reminds me of something Charlie said when I met him the other day, something about a long-lost cousin they had met somewhere but as the aunt was telling him, his grandma, Patience, told Auntie to shut up. The Cow and Calf are rocks on Ilkley Moor and—'

'Baht 'at?' asked Angela, with a smile. 'What does that mean?'

'Without a hat. Didn't you know that?'

'No, I had no idea what it meant. Now,' Angela became her usual bossy self, 'can you follow this lead?'

'Well,' said Edward, 'I'm going to see Charlie again on Wednesday. *Wuthering Heights* is quite near Ilkley so I can see if the library gives any clue as to when this flood occurred.'

'And,' Angela pointed out, 'that will give us a clue as to when the row was, because it took place five years earlier. If you give me the date of the flood, assuming there is only one possible one, I can go on with the other. It must have been a major national event if it was in the *Telegraph*.'

Chapter 7

1996

As he drove over the moorland road which was the shortest route from *Wuthering Heights* to Ilkley, Edward thought again about the snippet that Angela had read out, "… and Calf. It was fortunate that we did not go the following day for a great flood occurred in the town". It must surely be the Cow and Calf rocks on the side of Ilkley Moor. The area had been a popular tourist destination for many years. It is generally believed that *On Ilkla Moor Baht 'at* was composed on a chapel choir outing on the moor and Edward liked to imagine that the miscreants were seeking a quiet corner among those rock features. That landmark was linked to Charlie's memory of hearing from one of the aunts about a meeting at Ilkley, which was interrupted by a warning look from his Grandma Patience.

But first he needed to find out things which were in the public domain. He made his way to the library, an impressive Edwardian stone-built building where a fortunate meeting with a local historian gave him a great deal of information, which he was able to supplement from the local paper on microfilm.

That evening Angela was delighted to receive a phone

call from Edward. 'I've got it! I've got it!' His voice on the telephone seemed almost to suggest that he was jumping for joy, something Angela felt was rather out of character. 'They have the local paper on microfilm in the library and apparently, a real deluge was experienced at Ilkley on Thursday the 12th of July 1900, "… over the moor 5 inches fell in 90 minutes. Every road was a watercourse… bridges, culverts, trees and lamp posts all demolished". There are a lot of photos too; it does seem to have been a real disaster.'

'What's the date, did you say?'

'Thursday the 12th of July 1900.'

'Right, now we know that she, we are fairly sure it is your great-aunt Emily, who was "finally able to see him after five years" as she wrote almost certainly to my grandmother, so the row was in 1895. Now if I can access the *Daily Telegraph* for 1895… I think they are in the British Library or whatever; it's easy for me to go to London. Wait a minute – does that tie with the date of "the worst winter"?'

Edward laughed. 'That's easy. As I said before, as a geographer I know 1895 was a very hard winter, which was alluded to in that letter. The Great Frost it was called and it was the inspiration for the frost in *Winter Holiday*. Did you ever read that?'

'I loved Arthur Ransome's novels,' said Angela. 'That was actually the first one I read.'

Edward returned to the matter in hand. 'Now I've been thinking about the events in London "which have had their echo here". It must be spring. One of the letters from Leverford, as we now know it is, states: "The flowers which were developing in our little front garden have all withered". What a nuisance that they simply date their letters "Friday" and so on.'

'But what does Edith, my grandmother… I'm sure it must be her writing from Clarence Villas… mean about "the custom of 'prentice boys returning to their mothers at this time has fallen into abeyance"?'

'Oh that's Mothering Sunday, or Mid Lent Sunday. I have an old Book of Common Prayer here and now we know it was 1895 that will have been… hang on a second!' Edward dashed to the other room and found the prayer book. 'Here we are, the 24th of March.'

'So the storm… she writes "many of them would have been blown away or killed!" was spring 1895 and all then seems sweetness and light. It's later in the year when things start to hot up. It does narrow down the area I need to search. I shall go to the British Library tomorrow. The train service from Melcester is good and it deposits me right next to the library.

*

Angela caught the first available train that had the cheaper fare and entered the British Museum complex a little after 10.30. She had done some research in the library before and chuckled as she recalled Louis MacNeice's suggestion that the library was filled with "cranks, hacks and poverty-stricken scholars". Which, she speculated, was she? But it was intriguing how her ancestors, and those of Edward, were divided. Did that make her a crank, perhaps?

Approaching the issue desk she put her request, 'I would like to look at the *Daily Telegraph* for 1895.'

'I'm afraid all newspapers are at Colindale.'

'Where's that?'

'Colindale is on the Northern line – come out of the station and the Newspaper Library is on the left about a hundred yards down Colindale Avenue, a big brick building. You can't miss it.'

'Northern line – I'd best go to Euston then?'

'Yes – it's about twenty minutes out to Colindale from there on the Edgware route.'

She found her way easily enough. The library building reminded her of the town hall in Melcester, which was built in the 1930s; this would seem to be of similar vintage. The staff were remarkably helpful; she soon reached the relevant story. 'Oh!' she exclaimed aloud. 'So that's it!' The other readers glared at her, so she kept her thoughts to herself. 'My great-grandfather's brother… my great-great-uncle that is… was persecuted by the state, and perhaps also his family?'

★

Angela wanted to tell Edward immediately, but the thought of trying to use a public call box was off-putting. By the time she had looked up a couple of other things she wanted to check, it was late so it was eight o'clock before she reached home.

'I've got it!'

'What?' replied Edward, barely suppressing his excitement.

'I have found that quotation from the paper. It's fascinating to think what it might mean.'

'Did you get to the British Library?'

'Yes, but it was in another building in Colindale.'

'Where's that?'

'Edgware way. I had to use the Northern Line; fortunately it was not rush hour. Anyway, they were very helpful and produced the microfilm of the Torygraph. This seems to be the quotation; it is more or less like the last of your letters, or rather my grandmother's letter to your Great-Aunt Emily. "Let us hope that his removal will clear the poisoned air, and make it cleaner and healthier for all healthy and unvitiated lungs." That was in the *Daily Telegraph* for Monday the 27th of May 1895.'

'Unvitiated?' enquired Edward.

'I didn't know either,' chuckled Angela, 'so I looked it up. It's pure and uncorrupted.'

'But what is it all about?'

'The trial of poor Oscar.'

'Oscar?'

'Oscar Fingal O'Flahertie Wills Wilde.'

'Oh,' said Edward shortly, 'him.'

'Yes, but if those events have had an echo in Leverford and James is "abominable", we are inching our way towards "outing" your great-grandfather.'

'"Outing"?' Edward was baffled.

'Outing is disclosing a gay person's sexual orientation; James must have been gay, though the term would not have been used. There are innumerable slang and mainly abusive terms.'

'I know, I know. I don't like it, but at least the poor gays are not persecuted now. Wait a minute!' Edward was seized with a sudden idea. 'Did Emily meet James in Ilkley and who was "his friend"?'

'His partner perhaps?' Angela suggested.

'Would there be reports in the local newspapers of something? Presumably it would be in Leverford.'

'It may well have been hushed up, but you could try to find something; we know it was the same sort of time as Oscar's trial.'

★

Next day, Edward made his way to Leverford Central Library and up to the Local Studies room. He had spent quite a few hours there looking at the records of his ancestors.

The archivist was a lady of late middle age with grey hair drawn tightly back in a bun. Her clothes were grey, though relieved by a white blouse. She recognised him and her severe features relaxed into a smile that made her much more attractive. 'Oh Mr Simpson, how nice to see you! Is it the census records again?'

'No, Miss… I'm sorry, I've forgotten your name.'

She almost simpered. 'It's Katherine or Kate, Kate Austen.'

'And I'm Edward.' He stretched out his hand and she shook it. 'No, today I wanted to look at back copies of the *Express and Advertiser*.'

'Which year?'

'1895, probably the middle part of the year.'

'Ah now, until 1925 there were two papers. The *Express*, which supported the Conservative party and the *Advertiser*, which supported the Liberal party. The original copies are very fragile, and you need to make prior arrangements to use them; a few are too fragile to be brought out at all. We haven't yet got them on microfilm.'

'Oh!' Edward liked to do things now, or preferably sooner, as Mollie often suggested.

'But Mr Simpson, or may I call you Edward?'

'Please do.'

'As you are a valued member, as it were…' she laid her head on one side in an almost flirtatious manner. '1895, you say.' She consulted the catalogue. 'You are in luck. The *Advertiser* for that year is in bound volumes.'

'Well I support the Liberal Party, well the Liberal Democrats, so it could be a good start.'

He was soon sitting at one of the tables in the search room with the huge bound issues of the newspaper, turning the pages over. He had decided to begin at the beginning of the year and work steadily through. After an hour or so, he had just decided it was lunchtime and he would have a break when he saw what he was looking for. 'Oh no!' His exclamation was audible and brought Kate over.

'Is everything all right, Mr… err, Edward?'

'I suppose so, but… that's not really what I wanted to see.' He pointed to the news item.

★

Edward had hoped that what he had suspected was not in fact the case, but later that day he rang Angela to let her know. 'I've found him.'

'Who?'

'My great-grandfather.'

'You don't sound too pleased.'

'Well, it seems as though you were right. The gist of the newspaper report is this:

'A warrant for the arrest of Mr James Simpson, aged 46, a prominent local businessman who had a chain of pharmacies throughout the city… complaint made under oath and in writing that the defendant within the last two years at Leverford did commit an act of gross indecency with another male person, to wit, one Alan Royd, aged 24, a qualified pharmacist in the employment of Simpson… incited the said Alan Royd and others to commit sodomy…

'I carried on with my trawl of the newspapers – they were in bound volumes, not microfilm – and found he got *two years' hard labour*, the maximum sentence.'

'This was in 1895?'

'Yes.'

'So,' said Angela, 'when the 1901 census comes out in 2002, we can see where they were.'

There was no response from Edward.

'Are you there, Edward?'

'Yes, I can't quite take it in. I mean everyone said that my great-grandfather had died, though as I think I mentioned, I couldn't find any record of his death and when you came up with the idea, because of the apparent similarity with Oscar Wilde's situation,' he paused, 'that he was queer.'

Angela was about to correct his use of the term, but realised he was genuinely upset. 'I suppose it is hard to take in…' She paused. 'What happened to the chain of pharmacies after his disappearance? You said George Clarence took over.'

'He guided my grandfather at first. But my grandfather had trained as a pharmacist and took over fairly quickly. I found the record of his becoming an MPS.'

'MPS?'

'Member of the Pharmaceutical Society. My father told me he was very proud of that. So he ran the pharmacy side. From what I've gathered the business side was run by my great-grandmother, Patience Simpson, née Vaughan.'

'That's interesting.'

'What, the fact that a woman ran a business? I suppose so.'

Angela laughed. 'A feminist pharmacist! But could "his friend" who they met at Ilkley be James's partner?'

'You mean his… the man he was committing acts of gross indecency with? Ugh, I don't like to think about it.'

'What would you feel if it was a woman? Then it might be described as a night of mad passionate lovemaking.'

'That's different.'

'How? Oh, I'm sorry Edward, I'm being insensitive. I realise this is rather upsetting for you.'

Edward laughed. 'It doesn't matter. I guess I'm being a bit of a dinosaur. Anyway, I never knew him, so why should I be upset? I wonder what happened next?'

'Well, in a few years we should be able to track him down in the 1901 census and in the meantime we might try to find him through the Pharmaceutical Society perhaps.'

'I suspect he would have been struck off the register.'

★

After a few weeks, by which time he had accepted the situation, Edward attempted to use the records of the

Pharmaceutical Society and various trade journals, but without success. He kept in touch with Angela and other contacts were maintained because Henry and Joanna settled down together. They waited for the next census to be available and were eagerly anticipating it, the first to go online.

Epilogue

2002

'We're finally going to find out.' By November 2002, the system for accessing the 1901 census was in place. Angela and Edward were sitting at the computer in *Fairholme* and most of their generation and the next were clustered round.

'Well, go on, Angela.' Joanna spoke impatiently to her aunt. Initially, neither she nor Henry had any interest in the family history, but the discovery of James's homosexuality and consequent imprisonment had excited them.

'You mean,' Henry had said, 'that my great-great-grandfather…'

'Who is also my three times great-uncle,' added Joanna.

'Was disgraced for having sex with another man?'

'That's what happened in those days,' said Edward.

But now after all the investigation by Angela and Edward, then the frustration of the wait for the census to come online, they were to see where James had been just over a century ago.

'Shh, it's coming.' Angela held up her hand. There was silence.

'Well?'

'It's a good job we bought a whole lot of throws of the dice, or whatever they are called; there are hundreds, possibly thousands, of James Simpsons.' Angela was now wading through the data coming up on the screen. 'I've narrowed it down to Yorkshire and there are three, but two are labourers and the other a coal miner. I'll widen the search to all of England and the precise date of birth.'

She pored over the computer. 'There's a general labourer, a ship plate riveter, none of these seems likely... this could take for ever.'

'Do we know he was still alive?' Mark asked.

'He might have committed suicide,' suggested Matt.

'Don't be morbid,' said his brother.

'I was only—'

'Stop it, you two!' Mary put her foot down with her sons as, Edward suspected, she had done many times before. The tension grew as Angela pored over the screen. 'I need to be careful,' she said. 'We haven't many "goes" left.'

'Wait a minute,' put in Edward. 'Why not try his "friend", Alan Royd, who would have been thirty by then. There won't be as many Royds as Simpsons.'

There was a long pause. 'Aha!' Angela uttered a shout of triumph. 'Well done – isn't this them?' They crowded round the screen. This, which Angela later carefully copied out, was what they saw.

Name & Surname	Relation to Head of Family	Condition as to Marriage	Age last birthday	Occupation	Employer, Worker or own account	Birthplace
James Royd	Head	Widowed	52	Chemist & Druggist	Employer	Melcester, Melcestershire
Alan Royd	Son	Single	30	Assistant Chemist	Worker	Leverford, Yorkshire
Charles Lee	Servant	Single	18	Domestic servant	Worker	Islington, Middlesex

'James, right age and profession and born in Melcester.'

'So,' said Henry, 'he's changed his name to that of his partner and they are claiming to be father and son. Moreover he's "killed" his wife, who lived for another seventeen years. But where is this? What town?'

'Hindbridge. I'm not sure where that is… oh yes, yes. It's actually near Brungerley, where Albert's family were, where I met Jean Mason, just before her death. I don't think she said anything about James; I didn't ask.'

'It's far enough away from Leverford for there to be no gossip,' Edward added. 'It's easy enough to get to Ilkley from Brungerley or Leverford.'

'If I remember correctly,' interposed Angela, 'Emily may have had help from cousins; she wrote "… dear A and F" and then, "planning and scheming to be finally able to see him after five years".'

'And Emily wrote, "he brought his friend. I had always thought that he was a nice person…". So Alan went along too.'

'It must have been difficult for a middle-class Victorian lady to accept her father's gay lover,' suggested Joanna.

'I wonder what happened afterwards,' Edward mused.

'The 1911 census could be interesting but we are not allowed to see it for ten years.' Angela spoke with an air of finality.

Matt spoke, 'I wonder if Charles Lee was also gay?'

'Who's he?' asked Mollie.

'The servant to the other two.' Angela pointed to the screen.

'Oh, sorry, I'm being stupid. I can't really see the screen.'

'Islington and only eighteen… mmm. They might have been a ménage à trois.'

'Are there such things with gay men?' asked his mother.

'Oh yes, well today there are.' There was an uncomfortable silence, and then Matt exclaimed, 'Wasn't there an Uncle Charlie somewhere?'

'My uncle, a lot younger than this Charles Lee, not the same guy at all. I'm only thankful Uncle Charlie didn't live to see all this; he died three years ago. He couldn't have coped with it.'

Angela shot a quick glance across to Edward. In spite of their widely differing views on politics and religion, she had grown quite fond of, what was he, her third cousin… she was pleased to see her smile was returned. 'The end of a long road then?'

'Indeed,' Edward replied.

'Except,' Angela gave an almost conspiratorial grin, 'we can look for the dates of death of James and Alan, and look through trade directories and the records of the Pharmaceutical Society. More secret trysts for you and me, Cousin Edward.'

Letters found in Leverford and held by Edward

8, C. Villas
Tuesday

Dearest Cousin,

After what Mama declares to be the worst winter that she has known in all her fifty-two years, though how she can remember the weather when she was but a babe I cannot imagine, we now have had the most dreadful storm! It is a good thing that the old custom of 'prentice boys returning to their mothers at this time has fallen into abeyance, for I declare that many of them would have been blown away or killed! The area round our church here was littered with fallen branches of considerable size, and some of the pinnacles have come down. It is to be hoped that our dear Vicar has made suitable provision for such a calamity; I for one do not want to be involved in yet more sales of work to raise money for the fabric. Mother is still insistent that we support the home for unmarried mothers and one's time is not unlimited.

But I am neglecting to enquire after your health. I do hope you are well. Did the tempest affect your part of the world? One always imagines that Yorkshire receives much worse weather than the rest of the country. I suppose that Miss Brontë is, at least in part, responsible for this, though I have to confess that I find "Wuthering Heights" really too dreadful to read with enjoyment. By the bye, what does "wuthering" mean? I hope you have been able to get to all your ladies — are any of them very grand? I suppose some of the grandest are the wives of the mill owners. Do they have to wear their husbands' wares? No silk or satin, no linens or cottons, just woollens!

I suppose I am writing such silliness because I cannot decide whether to tell you my news. But there, I have said it, or rather written it, at least that there is news, or may be. Dearest cousin, you will remember that I told you that Mr Walker has been most attentive to me, well, it now turns out that he has seen Mama and been given permission to pay court to me. He is very handsome and I am quite flattered. It would be nice to have babies like dear A and F, Dora is getting quite big; she is walking and talking and even little Constance is beginning to sit up and take notice. It is delightful to be an aunt. "Auntie E" is what Dora calls me, but I want to be a mother, and I know Mama would like to see us all settled. Neither M nor L are showing any signs of wanting to get married. It doesn't really matter about G; being a man, he can cope. Mind you, as a single lady you seem happy enough, as indeed seems Auntie Lizzie. You both have your work of course.

There will be some drawbacks if I accept Mr Walker. He is a Dissenter and attends a church (or do they call it a chapel?) on the other side of the town. I do love our church here and we are privileged to have had some of the customs of the Medieval Church restored. My brother is very disapproving, saying it is like Rome. I daren't tell him what the Vicar asked me to call about the other day. He, the Vicar that is, hopes to establish a convent for nuns and wonders whether I might consider joining it!!!! Of course I couldn't and I wouldn't want to, even if I could. I suppose that has made me think about what I do want and be so anxious to accept Mr Walker. But the convent, if it ever comes about, will mean he is even more opposed to our church and in any case I fear he intends to make a

Dissenter of me. Certainly our children would have to be brought up in the faith of their father.

I envy you your independence at times. I said so to Mama one day last week. She smiled, but when I said that I thought that the ideal would be to be like you and Auntie Lizzie and have babies she went quite white, at first very angry, then sobbing bitterly. When I asked her to explain, she refused.

But I expect to follow a conventional path like she did, and, I expect, as you will.

I will close now and get this in the post this evening.
With every good wish,
Your affectionate cousin,
E

★

8, C. Villas
Wednesday

Dearest Cousin,

It seems a long time since you were telling me about your ladies and wondering whether Mr Walker, or Frederick, as I must now call him, would get down on one knee and propose — well, he has!!!!! At least he has proposed although he didn't get down on his knees or even one knee and protest undying love and devotion. It was all a little disappointing really, but he is handsome and Mama does hope that we shall all get married, with Papa not here to take care of us and my, at least, not having a trade or profession or any annuity. M shows no signs of having any gentleman friend and I'm sure that L is an old maid already. But then she at least has her own ladies to provide her with an income. He simply said stiffly that I must realise how he felt about me and that it would be highly desirable if we were to, Hrrumph (is that how one spells a clearing of the throat?!), come to an arrangement — it was as though he were engaging a servant! But there! It is done and we are to be married in the autumn at his church. I have agreed that any children will be brought up as Dissenters and he made it quite clear that he hoped that I would see my way to becoming one myself. I shall miss our beautiful church with our robed choir and our processions and, oh everything about our High Church ways. I haven't said I will "go over", but I fear that I must.

L is to make my dress and those of my... I hope you will be a bridesmaid, dearest. Let me know as soon as possible. Whitsuntide is nearly upon us and before long summer and then... we haven't fixed the date, but I hope it will not be too far beyond September 1st, as the weather begins to deteriorate after then. We are to go to the Lake District for our honeymoon. I am trying to persuade him that these might be the Italian Lakes — that would be so romantic — but he says that the journey is too long and he cannot afford to be away from the business for too long. But Derwentwater will perhaps be as grand as Lake Maggiore.

I hope so. Now let me know, but I won't take "no" for an answer! You will brighten up that gloomy conventicle. Imagine! It's called Providence!

With every good wish,

Your affectionate cousin,

E

★

8, C. Villas
Monday

Dearest Cousin,

Your last letter was so like a riddle. I could not make it out. I never read the newspapers and Frederick has expressly forbidden me to do so. I was trying to understand it — your letter — and he came in; he has assumed the role of father as well as lover, you know. He asked what I was reading and when I explained it was a letter that I could not understand he took it from me, with a brief "may I" that brooked no possibility of denial. He was puzzled at first and then sent a telegram; I believe it was to your house?

A whole spate of telegrams followed. Heaven knows how much this cost! And now, he has insisted that we do not write again! He says that your family is tainted. Dear E, what does this mean? I cannot accept it, yet I must. F is or soon will be my husband and I will have to obey.

In deepest sorrow,

Your most affectionate cousin,

E

*

An incomplete letter:

8, C. Villas
Sunday

Dearest Cousin,

Mama seems to defer to F in everything now. She accepts that we must not write and I am scribbling this in the scullery whence I fled on the pretext of making tea, for the servant has the Sabbath day off. I can hear their talk in the living room as I write; I am ashamed to say I have put my head to the wall. F is almost shouting at poor dear Mama and he has repeated this. I think I have transcribed it correctly; it is from the newspaper:

> Let us hope that his removal will clear the poisoned air, and make it cleaner and healthier for all healthy and unvitiated lungs.

I am now continuing my letter in my room, after having supposedly retired early with a sick headache. His repetition of the sentence above, *together with some sort of denunciation, which I heard only in part, was, I am sure, in the same newspaper article to which you allude, but F was associating it with your Papa. He shouted the words "Your Abominable Brother in Law". We must find a way to continue to write. I have an idea that A, who is older than F and—*

A Picture Postcard of The Lake District with a Stamp of King Edward VIII

Cheery greeting from the Lake District.
It is such a pity that you couldn't be here
with E and me.
Fondest love, E

Miss E. Simpson
16, St Andrew's Terrace
LEVERFORD
West Riding of Yorkshire

Letters found in Melcester and held by Angela

A fragment:

Post Scriptum: I'm delighted that you have found A and his new wife and that they are prepared to be friends. I know how upset you were when A and G had a row and he, A that is, walked out. Where is this place... in Lancashire, you say? Where cotton is King!

★

My dear Cousin,

I am sorry that I have been so long in replying to your letter. I will endeavour to answer it point by point.

After reading it I wished I could have rushed down to Melcester to see you, but as you know, my ladies are many and are rather demanding. None is very grand, though the new curate's wife is coming to see me next week. (I don't believe you think that we all wear nothing but wool in this county - do you?) Summer may be acumin in (did you have to learn that tiresome verse?), but it is not a time to sing "cuckoo". The new fashions will keep me busy for most of the next few months.

Tell me, has this handsome man got down upon his knees to you yet? But handsome is as handsome does and my advice is that, unless he be the latter, you don't accept him. You have confided in me; I shall tell no one unless you give me permission, say nothing about what I am about to write, I beg of you. I fear all is not well between Mama and Papa. He spends less and less time here at home and it is not, it would seem, that he is spending the time in the shop or the warehouse, for F was to begin his apprenticeship there this month, and Father has now said that it must wait, or that he must needs go elsewhere. It appears that he, Father, is going to his club, though where that is I cannot tell. Mama mopes a great deal and yesterday I found her in floods of tears, something most unlike her. Thankfully, I am well, though disturbed; the others are too young or heedless to be disturbed, and at least this dreadful winter does now seem to be over. We had long months of snow and ice but were spared the great storm you described in your letter.

So your church is really one of these ritualistic ones our Vicar so fulminates against! I cannot see what harm it would do to make the services of the Church a little more gay; they are so frightfully dull, and Father always insists that we go morning and evening, even when he does not, as he has not for some weeks now. With that and my teaching a Sunday School class, the day seems scarcely one of rest!!!!!!

I must confess that I did not know the meaning of the word "wuthering". I was sure that Harriet, our general, would know, having been brought up in the self-same valley as Haworth, where the Brontës lived. But when I asked her she simply said, 'Well, Miss, it means, well... wuthering, like.' But one of my ladies knew. It really means wild and stormy. But I am sorry you don't like the tale. It is so stirring and more true to life than all these novels that are written today. People cannot always "live happily ever after", though I hope that you may, dear " Auntie E"!!!! Have A and F had photographs made of the children? You must try to get me a copy of one, if so. Then I may see these - what are they? Cousins once removed, I think. Perhaps when I have completed the present rush I could take a little time away and come to Melcester. I would like to do that, and perhaps inspect your Mr W!!

    Fondest love from your ever affectionate Cousin
    E

★

16, St A Terr.
Friday

My dear Cousin,

    Felicitations! I hope you and your Frederick will be very happy.

    The flowers which were developing in our little front garden have all withered. It seems to mirror our family's situation, especially after a winter as hard as this has been. You will recall that I wrote that I believe that everything is not well with Mama and Papa. Now it has come to a head. And it has made Mama so unhappy and...

    This is the third or is it the fourth time I have tried to write this to you. I cannot really bring myself to tell you what I only dimly understand myself, but it seems that events in London reported in the Telegraph, which we take, have had their echo here. It was Mama's reading these reports that made her realise what Papa was. She is quite clever and, well, I suppose one could say that she put two and two together. She demanded the truth.

Heaven knows what will have happened by the time of your wedding. Do not plan for my being there. In haste and in sorrow.

Your ever affectionate Cousin

★

A fragment:

and Calf. It was fortunate that we did not go the following day for a great flood occurred in the town and I doubt we would have been able to catch a train home. All my planning and scheming to be finally able to see him after five years would have come to naught. He brought his friend. I had always thought that he was a nice person.

It is good that A and F allow themselves to be our intermediary and their children look delightful. I have put the photo in our album, tucked carefully away behind another one, for although Mama is still so angry with your Fred for forbidding us to even correspond, she would be quite vexed if she were to learn that I had been in touch with you.

A Picture Postcard of the Lake District with a Stamp of King Edward VIII

Warmest greeting from a not very warm Lake District. I hope you are being a good girl and doing as Mama says. Grandmama and Cousin E

Baby Angela Walker
Fairholme
MELCESTER

Roy

It was purely by chance that James saw the obituary. The name jumped out and it took him back to that day, over half a century earlier, at the beginning of the fourth year at Melcester Grammar. He had always spent his free time in school with Philip but his friend had left, and now he was on his own in the playground. He noticed another solitary figure. He had a slight resemblance to Philip and for a moment James imagined that it was him; he moved slightly forward with the beginning of a smile, then, realising his mistake, hesitated, the smile dying on his face. James knew he had never seen him before, although he wore the uniform of the Grammar School, but this stranger was advancing his smile undimmed. James returned the smile, if somewhat hesitantly.

'Greetings! I'm Roy.'

'I'm James.'

'Have you been here since Form 1?'

James nodded.

'I started in George Watson's in Edinburgh, then spent last year in Bradford. Now I'm here, and Mama says come hell or high water I'm going to stay here until I do School

Cert. She doesn't know it's called GCE now. I don't think it matters, because I'm going on the stage and intend being a great actor. What are you going to be?'

James had an answer for that question; his father expected it. He knew he wanted to go to university; he had to give a reason. Somewhat surprisingly, his mother had given him one; she had showed her husband the salary scales of the teaching profession. A graduate obtained a significantly higher rate than those who went to training college. His father was convinced; if James wanted to be a teacher and he had no objection to this, to university he should go. What he would not tolerate was his son's going to university without any career in mind. James was not sure about teaching, but if he could go to university he could then see what he felt. In the meantime there was peace at home.

'I'm going to be a teacher, I think.'

'You'll become a headmaster of course.' This was a statement, not a question. 'Of a top school, let's say Eton.'

'Umm. Err…' James was somewhat bewildered by this stranger; not the least of the reasons was his manner of introduction and his forthrightness. Most boys used their surnames and only when some degree of friendship had been established did they use Christian names. 'What's your other name? I'm James Law.'

'Donald Roy Stewart Forbes-McNair.'

James gulped. 'Roy McNair then.'

'Forbes-McNair, it's a double-barrelled surname, and you use both parts. Donald and Stewart you can forget. They're my grandfathers and they're both dead.'

'Which class are you in?'

'4A, I'm told.'

'But you can't be; I'm in 4A.'

'Why not? Will you not allow me to join your privileged group? Surely it is the headmaster who makes such decisions. I am of the correct age for the fourth year and I have the highest intellectual capabilities, so the top stream is most appropriate.'

'But you weren't there this morning in French and geography.' James spoke in an accusatory manner.

'No. The old goat asked me and my mother to come in at 9.30 and then kept us while he blethered on about the ethos of the school and how he hoped that I would fit in and how the Scottish system had much to commend it but how he thought that on the whole the English was better. Then he turned me out here and told me to go to Room D6 after the end of recess, or "break" as I believe you term it.'

'Yes. That's the physics lab. We have a physics class until lunchtime. We sometimes do experiments. Mr Marshall takes us for physics; he's a good sort.'

'I don't think physics relates much to the sort of life that I intend to lead. Unless, of course, I were ever to be asked to play the role of a great scientist in some play, one perhaps yet to be written. Is your most favoured subject physics?'

'No, I think it's perhaps English, or history.'

'Oh stick to English. It is a noble calling. Who knows? You may write the play about a great scientist. Then I shall take the leading role in it at the Old Vic. Of course it could be a play about a schoolmaster scientist like this Mr Marshall. You say he's a good chap?'

'Oh yes!' James became enthusiastic. But he was prevented from elaborating on the matter by the bell's ringing.

'Lead on, Macduff! You see I am not superstitious about the Scottish Play, my dear James.'

'I thought all actors were terrified of quoting from *Macbeth*,' James said as they moved back into the building. 'Mr Young told us when we did *Macbeth* in Form 2 that it was because the original actors were travelling magicians and that—'

'That may be so, my dear James, but we live in a scientific age and, whereas I do not consider myself in any sense a scientist, I nevertheless believe that we can draw on their understanding to illuminate aspects of our own lives. How can the mere utterance of words have any bearing on our actions, unless we choose them to? I look forward to an age when all superstition is dead. You are, I trust, an atheist, are you not?'

'Well…' James hesitated. He accepted unquestioningly the basic tenets of Christianity held by the Church of England, as was expected in the Law household, much as he accepted the science he was taught in school. After all, he reasoned, Mr Marshall could not demonstrate the structure of the atom any more than the Vicar could demonstrate the existence of God. His hesitation was seized on by Roy.

'Then if you *are* a believer,' he stressed the verb, 'you must hold it fervently; you must seek to convince me. We can argue it out into the small hours.'

James was about to say that his parents would not allow him to stay up so late, when they arrived at the physics lab. Before the class began, a few moments were spent in settling the new boy in. James was not altogether sorry that Roy was placed in another part of the lab – he found him somewhat disconcerting – yet he was at the same time rather drawn to the newcomer. He forced himself to concentrate on the work in hand, wondering yet again what real purpose the Wheatstone Bridge could have.

His thoughts were echoed by Roy as they came out together from the lab. 'I am inclined to agree with you, my dear James, about Mr Marshall's being a good chap, but he will never convert me. I cannot conceive of any purpose on earth, or in heaven, the existence of which I do not believe in, for a Wheatstone Bridge.' He almost spat out the last words. 'May I never have to suffer it again.'

Roy had been silent in class, quietly getting on with the minimum of work and speaking quietly and only when occasion demanded it, but this speech was delivered loudly in his rather high-pitched voice. In the playground at break there had been too much other noise for anyone else to hear; now most of the rest of 4A could hear and several sniggered audibly and nudged each other. At this moment the headmaster came up and buttonholed Roy.

'Ah! Forbes-McNair, there are just a couple of thing we didn't sort out this morning, so if you would come with me to my study. Err, Law!'

'Sir?'

'Could you come along as well so that you can show Forbes-McNair where the dining room is and explain the, err… procedures, to him.'

James had a moment or two to himself and time to think. There was something rather grand about Roy, his elegant disdain for convention, his habit of languidly laying his head to one side whilst gesturing with his hands palms held uppermost and the slight susurration in his voice. His thoughts were interrupted by a fellow fourth-former, Harry Brown, who had had to go to the staffroom, probably for some form of punishment, James imagined, knowing Brown.

'Tough luck on you, Law, getting stuck with that pansy.'

James was baffled. 'What do you mean?'

'Forbes-Macbeth, or whatever he calls himself. He's a pansy, should be given the once-over.'

'What's a pansy?'

'A nancy boy, a poof, y'know. My dad says they should all be locked up. He's told me to be on the lookout for them. Anyway, he's coming out of the Beak's now. S'long, mind what I said about him.' Brown scuttled off along the corridor in the direction of the dining room.

'How perfectly splendid of you to wait for me, old chap. The pangs of hunger are very strong now; I don't believe I could bear the strain of trying to locate the refectory.'

There was no one about just at that moment, so James was able to speak without fear of being overheard. 'Roy, can you...' he could not put it into words. 'I mean to say... your voice is...'

'I see. You are trying, somewhat inarticulately I fear, to say that my exuberance of speech and my extravagant manner are drawing attention. Attention which is not entirely of a favourable nature?'

James nodded. 'They, well, Harry Brown said that you were a...' he hesitated, '... a pansy.'

'Oh, that again. Well many of us actors are. Geilgud of course everyone knows about, but there are many others. It is quite acceptable in the theatre.'

'But what is it? What are pansies, nancy boys, poufs and so on?'

'Homosexuals, dear boy, homosexuals.'

'I don't... I think, that is... well, you ought to go gently; Harry Brown said that you ought to be given the once-over.'

'And am I to be frightened by this? Am I to change my behaviour to conform to Mr Brown's concept of normality? I do not follow fashion, I lead it. String along with me, Mr Law, and we'll do great things together.'

By now they had reached the canteen. The fourth-formers were on first sitting and most of the boys had taken their seats; James and Roy squeezed into the last remaining places on a bench in the corner near the further end of the room. James was glad of this; they could not have someone commenting on them from behind their backs. For the time being, at least, Roy was speaking in a moderate manner, enquiring about the names and interests of some of the others on the table. The main course, a stew with potatoes and green beans, was unexceptional, but when the second course arrived James shuddered slightly at his new friend's comments.

'And what, in the name of heaven, is that?' His finger trembled as it pointed towards a jug containing a pink viscous fluid, which had been placed on the table by one of the duty monitors. Another now brought the plate of chocolate sponge which it was to accompany.

'It's strawberry sauce, according to the menu, or pink custard if you like.'

Roy passed his hand over his brow, closed his eyes and groaned loudly. 'Oh my God! What benighted land have I reached! Pink custard!'

At this moment, Mr Cross, who taught Religious Education and was that day on dinner duty, came along. He was a pillar of the local Evangelical Church. 'You, boy!' He pointed at Roy. 'What is your name?'

'Donald Roy Stewart Forbes-McNair.'

'When you speak to a master stand up and address him as "Sir".'

Roy arose and stood languidly.

'Well? And don't slouch, boy.'

'I beg your pardon, Sir.' There was just the slightest trace of insolence in the enunciation of the last word.

'I asked you for your name,' Mr Cross almost snarled.

'I…' It was obvious that Roy had been about to comment that he had already done so, but thought it better not to. His tone was almost sweet as he repeated the quintuple form.

The master was not sure whether he was being fooled and looked hard at the pupil. 'Well, McNair, will you repeat to me what you have just said.'

'If you please, Sir, my surname is Forbes-McNair.' He paused, raising his eyebrows in conscious imitation of the other's refusal to proceed until the desired appellation were given. Surprisingly, the other complied.

'Forbes-McNair, then. Well?'

'I cannot for the life of me recall. One says so much in the course of a mere half hour that—' Roy seemed disposed to continue in a similar vein but was interrupted.

'What is the Third Commandment?'

James was surprised that Roy knew it and rattled it off. 'Thou shalt not take the name of the Lord thy God in vain: for the Lord will not hold him guiltless that taketh his Name in vain.'

'Good! I am glad that you are aware of the basis of our Christian faith. However, in your entirely unwarranted complaint about the colour of the dessert that Mrs Campbell and her staff have produced, you broke that commandment.'

'Oh my God!'

'Exactly!'

'But, Sir, there is a fundamental difficulty. I cannot take in vain the name of someone or thing in whom I do not believe. I might take your name in vain, were you to vouchsafe it to me. But I am an atheist and—'

'Come to the staffroom as soon as you have finished your meal, boy.' Mr Cross turned on his heel and went back down the room.

During the interchange the whole dining room had fallen silent, the silence spreading out from the table at which James, Roy and six other boys were sitting, as first the next table and then the succeeding ones had stopped their conversation, the boys fascinated, almost in the manner of those at a public execution, James thought. Mr Cross was not popular; his extreme evangelical Christianity found little support among the boys and his heavy sarcasm combined with severe punishments for the most minor misdemeanours made him the object of contempt mingled with fear. Somehow, those of the school present there in the dining room that day recognised that Roy had won a victory of sorts. Round one, perhaps, James meditated, but Mr Cross would eventually win; a teacher always did. The silence lasted a few seconds; all remained thunderstruck, some with open mouths. Then, suddenly, like a pent-up stream, the conversation burst out, with ever-increasing volume.

'Silence!' suddenly screamed Mr Cross; there was an almost hysterical note to his voice. 'You are all in silence; you are to eat your meal in absolute silence.'

The resulting calm was, James silently articulated to himself, as though a blanket had been thrown over a fire, no a better… what did one call it…? A better analogy was that the torrent continued under a sheet of ice that had suddenly formed at Mr Cross's behest. He remembered his fondness for descriptions of hell fire and thought that perhaps it would soon melt. He giggled quietly, and others followed his lead, for quite different reasons and not so quietly. It was unfortunate for James that Mr Cross, who had returned to his prowl of the room, had been looking at him at the very moment when he began to smile, and he evidently considered that James was furthering the impertinence shown by his friend. By now they had finished the chocolate pudding and its pink accompaniment.

'Right, that's it. Law, you too, and Forbes-McNair, go to the staffroom, go directly to the staffroom and wait for me there.'

If he heard the sotto voce "Do not pass Go, do not collect £200" from Roy and the rather louder giggle from James, Mr Cross gave no heed. As they passed through the ranks of the dining tables, James, at least, was aware of many admiring glances cast at Roy.

At the staffroom door they were met by Mrs Pickup.

'Yes, Law? Oh, this must be our new boy, Forbes-McNair. I'm Mrs Pickup and I shall be teaching you Geography. Welcome to Melcester Grammar. I hope that you will be happy here with us. I gather you have been in Bradford for the last year. Now what can I do for you?'

'I am delighted to meet you, Mrs Pickup. I am not very enamoured of your subject, but I am sure that you will be able to make it more exciting than has been my experience heretofore.' He concluded with a slight bow and made a gesture which almost suggested that he would kiss her hand.

Mrs Pickup did not extend her hand. 'Yes.' Her reaction was somewhat enigmatic. Charm this boy certainly had, but was he trying something on? She gave him one of her "hard looks" but mollified it with a smile and the slightest inclination of her head, which almost returned his bow.

James sought to rescue the situation. 'Mr Cross said we were to come here, Mrs Pickup. We misbehaved in the dining room.'

'You misbehaved, James? Good gracious me! But we all know Mr Cross has very high standards.'

'Actually, Mrs Pickup, it was I who was the guilty one.'

'Oh. I see.' She saw no reason to enquire about the nature of the offence, it might almost be unethical to do so, but Roy was determined to tell her.

'Mr Cross believes I have broken the Third Commandment; he regards it as a great sin. I was merely commenting on the disgusting nature of the sauce that accompanied the dessert.'

In spite of herself Mrs Pickup was intrigued. 'Tell me, for I don't know, I'm not testing you, which is the Third Commandment?'

'Thou shalt not take the Name of the Lord thy God in vain, for the Lord will not hold him guiltless that taketh His Name in vain.'

'I see.' Heavens, she thought, I must get out of this. She knew Richard Cross and his views; in an unguarded moment she had mentioned that she was herself an atheist and he now seemed to regard her as a sort of scarlet woman. Probably the boy had merely said "My God" or 'Christ' as a meaningless expletive, probably echoing his parents. Richard had overheard and then chosen to make an issue of it as he sometimes did with his colleagues in similar circumstances. She turned on her heel, bade the boys farewell and entered the staffroom.

At this moment Richard Cross himself arrived. 'Ah, Law, Forbes-McNair.' He paused for a moment. 'In the circumstances of your normally exemplary behaviour, Law, and that you may have been goaded into your action, which I can describe as nothing less than impudence, I am prepared to allow you to go now without further punishment.' He paused. James remained where he was. 'Well, boy. Go!'

'Please Sir, I am waiting for Roy. He's new and doesn't yet know his way around the school and the head said I was to show him around.'

'Humph! I suppose so. Wait at the end of the corridor then.' James moved away. Richard Cross turned to Roy. 'Now then, you say you are an atheist, well, I am not prepared to allow you to utter your views here. This school has a Christian foundation and as long as you are in it you will abide by its principles. I advise you to read your Bible, to pray and thereby avoid the certain damnation that will befall you unless you see the error of your ways. For your punishment you will come to my room, A6, at four o'clock and you will write out a suitable passage of scripture that I shall select. Now go, rejoin your friend and perhaps you may learn from him, he comes from a good Christian family.'

'But, Sir, my mother is meeting me and—'

'Silence. Otherwise your punishment will be more severe. Go!' The master turned and entered the staffroom.

Roy shrugged his shoulders and strolled down the corridor to where James was waiting. 'Did you hear what the old Bible-basher has told me to do?'

'It would have been difficult not to. I'm afraid his punishments are rather long. If you write quickly you should get out by about quarter to five, but you have to make sure that what you write is legible or he'll have you back the next day to do it again. Will your mother worry if you aren't home? Could I go round and tell her you'll be late?'

'I was to meet her in the teashop in the Market Place. We were to have had some species of celebration of my first day here. I shall go anyway; I cannot have my mama worried out of her tiny little mind. In fact, you come too; she suggested that I bring a friend.'

'Yes. I don't see why not, but I'll have to ring my mother first. Couldn't you ring up home? I mean let your mother know you'll be late?'

'Alas! I cannot use telephonic communication. The GPO has not yet provided us with a line, although we have the instrument, left by the previous owners.'

'There'll be the devil to pay when Cross catches up with you.'

'A curious choice of phrase. Do you believe in a personal devil as well as a personal God?'

James indicated that there were more pressing matters.

'Ah well, we can have a discussion on it at some future date.'

In such circumstances boys were allowed to use the telephone in the school office. Mrs Law was delighted to hear that James was to have tea with Roy and his mother, for she had been worried since Philip's departure by his apparent lack of friends.

★

So it was that at a little after four o'clock the two boys left, joining the ordered navy-blue uniformed throng that surged down into the centre of Melcester. Mr Cross meanwhile paced the floor of his room, his anger growing; no one had ever before defied him in this manner.

When they arrived at *The Kosy Kettle,* Mrs Forbes-McNair was already seated at a table in the window. She wore a coat that was of good quality but which had seen better days; it reminded James of the period about ten years ago when clothes were rationed and his rather fussy mother tried to "look her best", as she put it. The hat that Roy's mother wore was also, he recognised, of yesteryear's fashions, a rather small and angular creation with a pheasant's feather sticking out at a jaunty angle. As they approached she lifted her cheek to be kissed.

'Well, Roy dear, how was it? And is this one of your new friends?'

'This is James, Mama. We're in the same form, and he's been showing me the ropes.'

'How do you do, Mrs Forbes-McNair?'

'Delighted to meet you, James.' She accepted the proffered hand that James had extended to forestall her kissing him, and shook it firmly but somewhat vaguely.

'Roy, how many times must I ask you not to call me "Mama". And you too, James, please call me Ellen.'

'I'm not used to calling adults by their Christian names, Mrs Forbes-McN… err, Ellen. But if you want me to I'll…'

'Then that's settled, except that we wouldn't use the term "Christian". We aren't Christians, you see, as perhaps Roy has told you.'

'Yes, dear Ellen. And it's gotten me into a lotta big trouble, today.' Roy affected an American accent, obviously a private joke between them. He then gave an account of the lunchtime encounter with Mr Cross.

'Oh dear! Well, you're certainly right. I would have been worried, although I rather resent your use of the term "tiny little mind". I am a Master of Arts of the University of London and my mind is quite large. Yes, I know it's a catch phrase from… is it *The Goon Show?* No. Never mind, you can explain later. However, you are in a dilemma, and therefore so am I. It's too late to go back now, and you say,' she said turning to James, 'that this Mr Cross would have kept him in, even though I would have been waiting, and worried sick? Of course you could have asked James to come down here… but that might have been a bit of an embarrassment, I suppose.'

James nodded his head. 'Yes, he always does that, you have to sit there in that room and either do nothing, or write out long passages of the Bible. If you say anything, anything at all, he only keeps you longer. I've only been kept in once, but others are quite often, and it's always the same.'

'Well, I think we're going to have to try to find some compromise. I disagree with both the reason for it and the nature of the punishment, but we cannot ask for special consideration for Roy. Oh, yes of course,' she paused as the waitress had arrived, a short and rather plump woman, who almost appeared to be bursting out of her severe black uniform.

'What can I get you, madam?'

'I thought we'd all have the two-shilling afternoon tea. Don't worry, James, it's my treat. Then we'll sort out this problem.'

And so, over dainty sandwiches of cucumber and salmon paste and pink iced buns, Ellen Forbes-McNair outlined her plan. In what James imagined was a characteristic approach to such matters, she paid lip service to the idea that a joint decision was being taken, whilst nevertheless imposing her own views. 'There can be no argument that you should not undertake some equivalent punishment, but if you were to go tomorrow…' she paused, 'I know, we'll present him with a fait accompli. You will go in tomorrow with a piece written out, which I shall certify as having been done by you. I shall write a letter to the headmaster advising him of the facts, and also letting him know, very discreetly, that I consider this approach by a member of his staff to be unacceptable, in particular this imposition of what I regard as superstitious ideas.'

'Ellen, you're not going to make me write out a whole chunk of the Bible are you?' Roy's tone was plaintive. 'You can't, you don't believe it.'

'In the form we have it today, Roy, it's very beautiful English prose. And it's a fascinating record of history and mythology. I believe that. I just don't believe the interpretations that are put on the events recorded in it, either by the writers of the various books of the Bible, or the theologians.'

James listened spellbound. Although his parents were not what would be later known as "fundamentalists", they accepted the Bible as the inspired word of God in an entirely unquestioning way. His mother was well versed in it and could usually be relied upon to provide an apposite quotation in any circumstance. Right now, he would guess that she would quote St Paul. What was it? *Whatsoever things were written aforetime, were written for our learning; that we through patience and comfort of the Scriptures might have hope.* It would be pointless to quote it here; even his mother would not try to force her religious views on new acquaintances; she would consider it rude. But what was Mrs Forbes-McNair saying?

'Well, of course, if you were to write out a passage from a good socialist treatise, he might object so strongly that we should have to… I know! You can write out something from the *Song of Solomon*. It's really a love poem, not like the rest of the Bible at all, although the editors try to see it as being a metaphor for the relationship between Christ and the Church. It's clearly nothing of the sort. There's one line, I think I've remembered it correctly: *My well beloved shall lie all night betwixt my breasts*. He cannot object to it because it is the Bible, and you will learn a little of your literary heritage. And next time, moderate your speech to suit the occasion. It's the only way to get on in our society.'

This time James was genuinely shocked. First there had been mention of socialism as though it were to be commended; in the Law household socialism was an utterly damnable creed. Then an adult had actually described well… sex. Of course, James had heard the usual types of "dirty jokes", but one never imagined that adults ever talked about such matters. Any references to such would have merited the severest condemnation, at least as far as James's parents were concerned.

'I think we're quite baffling James,' said Ellen. 'Our household is a free-thinking, socialist one. What's yours?'

'Well,' said James, 'we go to St Philip and St James Church every Sunday and on all the major festivals, and my parents always vote Conservative. My father is the Secretary of the Constituency Party and he stood for election to the Council last year,' he added proudly. 'Not that he wanted to be elected, he was just keeping the flag flying in a Labour stronghold, you know.'

'Of course I would disagree with them in almost all aspects of their belief. But it is good that they have definite views. In the seventeenth century there was a Christian of a more independent turn of mind than most, a man called George Fox, the founder of the Society of Friends, the Quakers. Have you heard of him?'

James shook his head, but then recalled something. 'Isn't there a Quaker church in a back street behind the Market Place?'

'There is indeed; I passed it this afternoon in a little exploration I made of the centre of the town. But it isn't really a church, it's a meeting house, and that street is Meeting House Lane. It was the name that attracted me. I was a Quaker once, and there are certain things about Friends that I still find very appealing. To go back to Fox, he once said to someone who quoted others' views and would not state her own, "But what canst thou say?" Well, James, what canst thou say? You said that you go to church; you didn't say that you were a Christian. Are you one? Your parents vote Tory, you can't vote until you're twenty-one, but what are your own political beliefs?'

'But isn't everyone really a Christian? I mean socialism is really a sort of Christianity, isn't it? Love thy neighbour and—'

'Oh no! It's quite different. Christianity is based on the belief in a supernatural agency that intervenes in the world. Think of the Creed, which presumably you recite at each service. I'm afraid I utterly reject that and—'

'Mama dear, Ellen. Isn't this just a teeny little bit too heavy for a wet Monday evening? A little social chit-chat might be more appropriate, and you're terribly good at that.'

Thus Roy steered the conversation away from religion and politics. Soon Ellen was enquiring about his parents' occupations and at least giving the appearance of listening politely. James felt more comfortable with this; he was not sure which aspect of the former conversation had disturbed him more, the freely expressed views so contrary to those of his own home, or the way Ellen so calmly treated him as an adult. After they had finished tea and Ellen had paid the bill they went out together into the rapidly darkening Market Place.

'Well, James, it has been lovely to meet you. I think we must be off to our respective homes now. We'll always be delighted to see you, and next time I shall demand to know what thou canst say.'

★

It was six o'clock when James arrived home to be met by his mother in the hall.

'Where did you go for tea, their house?'

'No, Ellen had been doing some shopping and had arranged to meet Roy in *The Kosy Kettle*. We had afternoon tea. It was nice, thin cut sandwiches and iced buns.'

'How much was the tea? I hope that you offered to pay, although I presume that your offer was refused.'

'Two shillings. I couldn't offer to pay; I only had about tuppence halfpenny.'

'I suppose so. And if they invite you… is Ellen Roy's sister? I thought you said on the phone that you were meeting his mother?'

'Ellen is his mother, she wants—'

'James I'm ashamed of you. I thought your father and I had brought you up to be respectful to your elders and betters. What would Mrs McNair say if she were to hear you using her Christian name?'

'She told me to, and she doesn't want it to be called a Christian name. They're socialists and atheists so that—'

'Socialists! Atheists! Oh James, I don't know whether I want you to be associating with such people.'

'But Mother—'

'I'll discuss it with your father.' She spoke these words with an air of finality and James knew that it was futile to argue. He regretted now that he mentioned either the manner of address that Roy's mother suggested or her views on politics and religion. He should have known what the reaction would be. But voices were never raised in the Law household and eventually there would be an agreement, even if it meant that James had to do something he really would have preferred not to do. Surely, though, they would not want him to give up his new friend?

Supper was, as always, promptly at seven o'clock, almost immediately after his father arrived home.

'I hope you're going to want this, James,' said his mother as she placed a large helping of mashed potato onto the plate where two tiny lamb cutlets and a spoonful of green beans already sat.

'Why wouldn't James want his food, Jane?' enquired Andrew Law. 'He always has a healthy appetite.'

'Well, he's been out to tea. A very nice afternoon tea costing two shillings of someone else's money.'

'A friend at school invited me to *The Kosy Kettle*, or rather his mother did.'

'Jane, we must invite that boy around here, or can you reciprocate by taking him and James out to a café sometime?' Andrew Law had an almost fanatical desire "not to be beholden to anybody", and insisted on calculating down to the last halfpenny how much he owed any who did him favours. Christmas and birthday presents had to be chosen to be of similar worth to that previously given by the intended recipient. Jane had had to trudge round shops, first to discover the cost of the gift and then to find something of comparable price. A careful record was kept from one Christmas to the next to enable this to be done. Jane did not resent this; she too firmly believed that it was wrong to be in any sort of debt.

'We must, of course, Andrew, you are quite right. But I am unhappy about James continuing to associate with his family.'

'Aren't they a respectable family? Where do they live, James?'

'Copthorne Crescent, number 24.'

'That's a very good neighbourhood. What is wrong, Jane?'

She pursed her lips. 'They are atheists and socialists and Mrs McNair wants James to call her by her Christian name, and yes, James, I shall continue to call it a Christian name, that's what it is properly.'

'I know some good chaps who are socialists. There's that man who's councillor for Fairview Ward, Bernard Lawson. Got some crazy ideas, believes that nationalisation is a good thing, I ask you, when you look at the railways! But he's an absolutely tireless worker for those in his patch who've got problems, and you know how many problems there are in an area like that. But we can't agree with him, stands to reason. As for the other, well, that's your mother's thing. Seems to me though that a chap's got to have some sort of belief, some rules to live by. Can't hold with people making too much of a parade of their religion, and it seems to me that's just what these militant atheists are doing. Their religion is no religion, if you see what I mean. But I don't see why James shouldn't be friends with the lad, just as long as he stands up for what he knows is right, the Tory party and the Church of England. Eh?' Mr Law chuckled heartily and slapped his son on the back.

'If you say so, dear. But hold fast to that which is right, James. Don't imperil your immortal soul. And if Roy comes here to tea, as he must, I will have to ask him to call me Mrs Law; I think it is only right and proper that he should, whatever his mother thinks.'

★

Next day Mrs Forbes-McNair arrived at school five minutes before her son and demanded an interview with the headmaster. A few minutes later, Mr Cross was seen entering the head's study. All three emerged together a little before nine o'clock. The head, in his billowing academic gown, was all smiles; he seemed almost to be flirting with Roy's mother, who was maintaining a somewhat detached attitude. The third was stony-faced and silent. Nothing more was said about the punishment and in class, Mr Cross was very wary of Roy, who in his turn was always charming.

The apparent victory of Roy over the hated Mr Cross secured him a place in the affections of the boys of the Grammar School. One or two of them did make comments using "poofter" or similarly pejorative terms, but they were quickly overruled and he became a loveable eccentric, rather than a figure to be mocked or physically abused. Roy never attempted to deny the charge, merely smiling and occasionally making a comment such as, 'If you say so, dearie!'

When Harry Brown renewed his verbal attack on James as an associate of "that pansy", he was firmly put in his place.

'Forbes-McNair's all right, and Law's his mate, so you leave them alone.' There was an implicit threat in this statement from Hadlow, the rugby captain.

*

James's parents insisted on a reciprocal gesture as soon as was possible, so on the Friday afternoon following the Monday tea at *The Kosy Kettle*, Roy and James were on the way for tea at the Laws' home. On their way James asked Roy about homosexuals. He received a somewhat vague and evasive answer.

'Well, they are men who dress as women and, well, you know.' Roy waved his hands about in a way that meant little to James. 'I'm not one, you know, whatever Brown thinks. But we approach your ancestral home. You say I must address your dear mama as "Mrs Law"? Of course it shall be so, and no, I shall not discuss politics or religion with either her or your dear papa.'

The tea at the Laws' house went well, for Roy exercised all his charm and even the rather stuffy Andrew accepted him as James's particular friend.

During that term James and Roy became firm friends, having tea in each other's houses and going to the cinema on Saturdays. But whether it was hell or high water, Roy had not stayed to do GCE; indeed for some unexplained reason he left at the end of that term. He never wrote to James as he had promised; gradually the memory faded.

*

James saw the obituary in a local newspaper that someone had left on the train. There could be no doubt: there could be no one else with the name Donald Roy Stewart Forbes-McNair. But he had been a stockbroker, not an actor, and his obituary mentioned his "years of unstinting service" as secretary to a golf club in a small Surrey town. So much, thought James, for his intention to be a great actor. It seemed unlikely that a man with socialist views would have been involved with such a group, although there was no mention of any political affiliation. The last section of the obituary intrigued him, "Mr Forbes-McNair never married", the usual way of indicating that the deceased was gay.

Helena

Helena sat outside *The Kosy Kettle*; an absurd name, she thought, but they did make a good pot of tea and the homemade scones were delicious, especially when they were served with strawberry jam. This came in a small individual dish and was claimed as "home-made". Today, she decided to try bara brith, which she remembered from childhood holidays in Wales. She understood that the name means "speckled bread"; it was rather good, she discovered. It was pleasant sitting out on the main street of Melcester on a fine late summer day, although the tables crowded onto the pavement were, she supposed, intended for the smokers, now exiled from the interior.

'Have you got a light, love?' The speaker was one of two young women who had arrived shortly after Helena, had dumped their bags down, and taken over the next table. Helena shook her head.

'I ought to give up too, but you know how it is. Tomorrow… but tomorrow never comes?'

Helena smiled weakly. The women were not young really, except that to her almost all people were young. 'Actually I never smoked.'

'Really? It was part of growing up in our patch.'

What would her parents have thought of the smoking ban, she wondered? Both had been quite heavy smokers, though she herself had somehow never got around to it. Last Thursday, which had been a grey drizzly day, she had sat at one of the inside tables and watched the smokers huddled under the flapping awning that gave some shelter for the outside tables. It was difficult to imagine Mother or Father sitting there, but to light a cigarette was almost the first thing they did in a café, after they had taken off hat and coat and sat down. In fact, Mother usually kept her hat on. Today, all the customers of *The Kosy Kettle* who were outside were smoking; she felt left out somehow.

But being left out was something that she had come to accept. She was the "tail end" of the family, born in the earliest days of World War II to parents who were themselves born at the very end of Queen Victoria's reign; she always assumed it was a failure of contraception. Her three brothers had taken jobs directly from grammar school, ones which did require at least School Cert. and which offered promotion, office jobs... white-collar workers one called them, she believed. Maureen, her only sister, the first born and fifteen years her senior, had worked in various shops in the town, both before and after her marriage. She had not tried for what was called the scholarship, had remained in the elementary school and left at fourteen. Helena had passed the eleven-plus, went to the Girls' High School and had eventually gone to a teacher training college in London, where she had found a job in a primary school. At each stage her parents had to be persuaded; that after O level she should go into the sixth form, that she should then go to college and that she should remain in the capital after obtaining her teaching qualification. To convince her parents on the last she stated that promotional opportunities were greater in London, although that was not something they really accepted; both expected her to follow Maureen's example, marry and settle down in Melcestershire. It would be wrong to suggest that her parents cast her off because of this and she always returned for Christmas and family events, but she was rather removed both physically and emotionally and since the death of her siblings; although her nephews and nieces sent Christmas cards and even visited her from time to time, it was obvious this was just a duty.

She had achieved success, becoming deputy head of a large and successful primary school in a London suburb that was neither a "leafy suburb" nor a "difficult" area. She had retired as the new millennium dawned and returned to Melcester in order to… to what? Part of the rationale was to raise a little capital. The sale of her flat, a spacious two-bedroomed one in a 1930s block in what had become a "desirable" area of West London, had enabled her to buy a house in her home village in Melcestershire. None of her family now lived in the area and few in the village remembered them. The additional capital, invested as suggested by a financial advisor, meant that she had money for travel, which she had always enjoyed, although she had usually seemed on the fringe of the groups she had joined for various tours of the continent and beyond. Most of the others were couples and politely passed the time of day, invited her to sit at meals with them. Sometimes they had suggested that she might accompany them on additional excursions, but she had always refused.

Now, her life had settled into a humdrum monotony. The village library, which had not existed in her childhood, had now closed and so she took the bus into Melcester, usually on Thursdays, which was market day. Her mother had done the same, although she often went to Boots Book-Lovers' Library.

'The public library is so full of such unsavoury characters,' she had claimed.

It had fallen to her to clear the house after her mother's death; she had found several books with the familiar green shield logo of the Boots' Library with a cancellation mark and recalled her mother's buying these "rejects"; they were a shilling each, she recalled. One was a particular joy to find, an early Barbara Pym, now long out of print. She could not remember her mother's buying that, still less could she imagine her really enjoying Miss Pym's subtle humour. Like Maureen, her mother's taste had been limited to simple romantic fiction and "home-building" books. Her brothers read only what was necessary for their work. Helena loved the classics of English literature and had achieved 80% in A-level English Literature and high marks in History and French. Miss Appleby, the headmistress of Melcester High, had tried to persuade her to make a late application for university.

'With those marks, Helena, you would be able to get into university. I know you want to teach, but a university graduate earns more than one from a training college.'

She knew this but also knew that it had been a struggle to persuade her parents to consider a two-year college course. The university route with a three-year degree course and a postgraduate training year would never have been accepted. She had been in primary school teaching so it was not really possible to teach the main works of English Literature. She had once tried to interest Maureen in *Pride and Prejudice*.

'Just listen to this,' she said to her sister one day, pulling the book down and opening it. Hurriedly flicking through the pages she rejected the well-known opening: "It is a truth universally acknowledged…" in favour of:

I was very much flattered by his asking me to dance a second time. I did not expect such a compliment.' When Jane and Elizabeth were alone, the former, who had been cautious in her praise of Mr Bingley before, expressed to her sister just how very much she admired him. 'He is just what a young man ought to be,' said she, 'sensible, good-humoured, lively; and I never saw such happy manners! – so much ease, with such perfect good breeding!' 'He is also handsome,' replied Elizabeth, 'which a young man ought likewise to be, if he possibly can. His character is thereby complete.

'You see,' she said to Maureen, 'it's about love and romance and—'

'OK; I'll try it.' But a few days later she returned it saying it was boring. Later she had watched the televised version, but she was not too struck with that.

Helena became aware that one of the women was speaking. 'I'm sorry, I was miles away.'

The other smiled. She had a tattoo on her neck; her hair was untidy and hung in greasy strands. She wore a denim jacket as well as the ubiquitous jeans. Her mother's comment about the users of public libraries came back to her: "unsavoury characters".

'I said was you a teacher? All them books.' She pointed to the hessian bag that Helena had picked up in India and which she used for carrying books to and from the library.

'Well, I was a teacher, I'm retired now of course, but I love books.'

'Oh I like books, d'ya know, when I was at school I hated English Lit, but I got hold of this.' She waved what appeared to be a romantic novel. 'Well, this girl, well a woman really, same sort of age as me, she's lost her husband in a terrible accident and had never at her age expected to find love again, when this man comes along and sweeps her off her feet. I wish it'd happen to me. I could do with a man in me life again.'

'Did your…' Helena hesitated, he may not have been a husband, so many people didn't get married nowadays, 'did your partner meet with an accident?'

'My old man? He nearly did. Well, it wouldn't have been an accident, I nearly murdered him.'

'Oh dear. Was he…?'

'When I learnt he was having it off with that blonde in the *White Lion*, I hit the roof. But I controlled myself, told him to get out, then packed all his stuff and left it in the garage for him to collect. I did think of making a bonfire of it, but he wasn't quite that bad.' She shrugged her shoulders.

The other women spoke. 'He was a good-looker all right, was your Tony. And he'd be good in bed…'

The first woman came back suspiciously. 'How do you know? Did he have you too?'

'Keep your hair on. No, he didn't! Anyway I don't know why you want another man. I've had enough of them. Y're better off on your own.'

'I like a bit of company; even if the guy is a shit. Not just sex, someone to watch telly with, someone to shout at when life gets you down.'

Some time ago Helena had watched a play on television where two people of '*un certain age*' had met and begun a relationship. What is '*un certain age*'? She smiled; it was really saying that you were old but not past it. Both the protagonists were widowed, so the situation of the woman in the play was not comparable with her own. It had happened here, inside *The Kosy Kettle* last spring.

She had been sitting at the window table, watching the world go by, when her thoughts were broken by a gentle cough.

'Err, excuse me.' The speaker was a tall, well-dressed man of perhaps her own age. He was wearing a brown tweed jacket, a pale yellow shirt and a contrasting tie.

'I wonder if I might borrow the sugar basin? There isn't one on my table.'

What had prompted her to say what she said next, she was never sure. 'Why don't you join me here? There is a nice view.'

'That would be very kind of you.' He brought his half eaten slice of Bakewell Pudding and cup of coffee; she observed that he drank it black. He extended his hand, 'Andrew, Andrew Bradshaw.'

She extended her own hand and their fingertips met. 'Helena Clarkson.'

'Pleased to meet you, Helena.'

She murmured something in return.

Their conversation proceeded easily, dealing with only ordinary everyday matters and their respective tastes in all sorts of aspects of life, including entertainment.

It was not every Thursday; she sometimes went into Melcester on other days of the week, but there must have been perhaps half a dozen meetings at *The Kosy Kettle* before one day Andrew had asked, 'Do you like opera?'

'Grand opera, do you mean? I love G&S but…'

He chuckled, 'I suppose I mean grand opera. There's a touring company at the Victoria Theatre next week and one of their offerings is *Carmen*. That was classed as opéra-comique.'

'Comic? I thought it was a dreadful tragedy. She dies, doesn't she?'

He nodded. 'It's because it has spoken dialogue that it was so classified. Anyway, I've got tickets for the first night. Would you do me the honour of accompanying me?' He gave a little bow.

It was the first of several outings. There were visits to other theatres, meals in expensive restaurants and on one occasion he drove her out into the Peak District where they had afternoon tea in a delightful village and later watched the sun go down from a point high above a valley. There was no physical contact beyond a gentle kissing of her hand, after which he looked up with a boyish grin and chuckled before he let her hand fall.

They had never exchanged addresses or telephone numbers. At each meeting they had made arrangements for the next one. He met her at the bus station where she arrived from the village and he escorted her there after the evening was over. The trip to the Peak District was different. 'I've got the car next Thursday,' he had said. 'Let's go out for a day in the country. Can I pick you up at your house?'

She had given him her address and promptly at the agreed time he was there in a sleek dark blue Rover 25. It was the last time they met. When he dropped her, he said, 'It's been a wonderful day. I hope you think so?'

'It has indeed. I haven't been there for years and where we had tea was a lovely café.'

He held her hand longer than usual and there was a wistful look as he relinquished it. Only after he had driven away did she realise that they had made no arrangements for another outing. Of course he had her address now, so perhaps he would write, or even telephone; she was not ex-directory. But nearly a year had passed and there had been no contact. Helena guessed he was a married man and indeed she imagined that the Rover had had a faint reek of perfume. Andrew Bradshaw was not listed in the telephone directory.

A cackle from the next table brought her back to the present. 'Here, Missie, teacher!'

'I'm sorry, what did you say?'

'I said I bet you kept your men in order didn't you? Like the kids you taught!'

Andrew had been the only person in her life that had been her man; she had not kept him in order. 'I did try, I did try.'

'Good on yer!'

She was suddenly startled by a hand on her shoulder. 'Helena, I hoped I might find you here.' It was Andrew.

The Lost Phone

I am always wary of those who make comments such as, "it was all intended", but sometimes the oddest things can have unexpected consequences for good or ill. It was a spur-of-the-moment decision to travel up to London from my home near Honiton in Devon; I was intending to visit the Tate Modern to see a new exhibition and hoping to go to a play in the West End. I had booked myself a night in a modest bed and breakfast, as return travel in the evening is limited. It is usually possible to find a single seat in a theatre, especially midweek and off season. Having retired with a reasonable index-linked pension I could indulge myself in these ways and, since I lost my wife a couple of years ago and had no children, I had no reason not to. I had travelled the route so many times that I didn't bother to watch the passing countryside and had dozed off, when with a start I realised that we were pulling out of Woking and that we would arrive in Waterloo in about half an hour. It was then that the phone began to ring, a straightforward *brr-brr*, not one of these fancy ones with a tune, but its continuing made it almost as irritating. Why doesn't someone answer it? But it was on the seat on the other side of the aisle and no one occupied that now. I tried to recall who had occupied that place.

'That your phone ringing, mate?' The speaker was the man in front of me.

'No, someone has left it there. Has he… she… gone to the loo?'

'It was a she, a middle-aged lady, got out at Woking.'

The phone had stopped ringing; evidently the caller had given up. I picked it up. It was an ordinary small phone rather than one of the absurdly named smartphones. As I looked round for the guard, or train manager as they are now called, it began to ring again. The display showing *Accept Call* indicated which button to press. I am a bit of a numbskull with technology, but that was easy.

'Hello!'

'Is that you Joyce? It doesn't sound like you.' The voice suggested an older, educated woman; her manner was almost accusatory. 'I've been ringing this for ages, first it was… what did it say? Anyway, you weren't there. Then it rang and rang and you didn't answer.'

'It isn't Joyce, I'm afraid…'

'Oh? Have I got the wrong number?'

'I don't think so. Your friend Joyce left her phone on the train when she got off at Woking. I was just about to find the train manager, the guard you know, and give it in.'

'Woking? Why would she get off at Woking? She is meeting me at Waterloo and I was ringing to tell her that I was a bit delayed…' She continued talking but the noise of the train running over the points and the announcement that we were arriving at Clapham Junction drowned her words.

When conversation became possible I interrupted her. 'Look,' I said, 'we're at Clapham Junction and we'll be in Waterloo in about ten minutes. If we meet there I can give you the phone and you can find Joyce.'

'Where shall we meet?' She sounded rather less forceful now.

'Under the clock? I know it's a cliché but it does make things simpler. What time can you get there?'

'I'll be there in about half an hour. My name's Valerie, well, everyone calls me Val. I'll be wearing a purple coat.' She giggled. 'When I am old I shall wear purple.'

I forced a laugh. 'I'm Stuart and I am wearing a blue anorak.'

I wondered whether, in all the hustle and bustle of the station, we should be able to find each other, but when Val appeared there was little doubt. She had an authoritative air and strode down the platform, weaving her way between the other passengers. Her purple coat, which was not fastened, was worn as though it were a royal robe – "… a certain rich man who was clothed in purple and fine linen and fared sumptuously every day…" – what was that from? As for faring sumptuously, she was slim and beautifully proportioned. She strode up, holding out her hand. 'Stuart?'

I extended my own hand. 'I am; you must be Val?' She shook it vigorously. 'Here's Joyce's phone. It's switched off now.'

She took it and slipped it into her handbag.

There was an awkward silence, which I broke. 'Well, shall we have a coffee or something before we part, or do you need to be going?'

'I was rather hoping that you might help me find Joyce.'

'Oh, well… err, I was going to an exhibition at Tate Modern and then I hoped to a theatre.'

'I see!' There was more than a hint of disapproval; I felt as though I were at school again.

'I could help, but—'

'Good. Now let's have that coffee and plan our strategy.' She led the way to *Carluccio's*. I would have preferred *Caffè Nero*, not the least of the reasons being that I have a loyalty card, but it seemed better not to argue with Val.

'Now!' she said when we were installed in the café and were enjoying coffee and pastries. 'It seems to me that we need to get the train back to Woking and follow the trail, before it goes cold. Was Joyce wearing anything distinctive?'

'I really cannot remember anything about her. It was only after she had got out and the phone began to ring that I realised anything unusual had happened; I wasn't even sure whether the person was male or female.'

'Umm. I wish she had said *why* she was going to get off at Woking before she lost her phone.'

'She probably would have done. I don't suppose she intended to lose it.'

Val permitted herself a slight smile. 'No, of course. She was always losing things when we were children.'

'Oh, so you are…?'

'Sisters, yes. She is a couple of years younger than me. Though she has let herself go rather, and people might imagine she is older. If we go to Woking we might just find her.' The last words were spoken in an authoritative way as she drained her coffee and led the way to the booking office. 'Two returns to Woking, err, wait a minute,' she turned to me. 'Do you have a railcard?' I produced it; she had her own. 'Seniors, that is.'

She was silent on the short journey and I sat there, wondering what the hell I had let myself in for. Then we both spoke together.

'She'll have got some idea in the head and then whatever happens…'

'That's the oldest mosque in Britain and…'

'She might have decided to get off and look at that; it would be just like her.'

'But the mosque is the London side of Woking; she wouldn't have seen it, because she got off before the train reached there.'

The train stopped at the station and we got off. Val led the way. At the barrier we stopped and fumbled for our tickets. 'Excuse me,' she said as we passed through the barriers. 'What happens if someone with a ticket to London from Salisbury gets off here?'

The railwayman looked surprised. 'Well, if he put his ticket through the barrier it would be returned. Why do you ask?'

'My sister got off at,' she turned to me, 'what time? She was getting the 10:21 from Salisbury and was to meet me at Waterloo at 11.52.'

'That stops here at 11.15,' interposed the railwayman.

'Did you see anyone get off who was a bit agitated, about my age? A woman.'

'Sorry ma'am, but have you any idea how many come through here every hour, even every five minutes?'

'Hang on,' this was from a female rail employee, 'was she wearing a beige coat, grey hair, a bit all over the place?'

'That could be Joyce. Why? Did you see her?'

'A lady like that at 11.15 or so came off a train on Platform 2, asking about Brookwood Cemetery. Wanted to know about trains to there.'

'And are there? Trains to the cemetery?'

'Yes, five minutes down the line and there's an entrance opposite the station. She'd just missed the 11.19, but there was one at 11.30; I guess she caught that, but I can't be sure.'

'Right! We'll follow her. C'mon!' Val turned to me, 'We'll need tickets to Brookwood. When's the next train?'

'Nineteen minutes past, platform five. It's the Basingstoke train.'

Within a few minutes we were on that train. I felt drained. Val was an exhausting person to be with and she had somehow taken me over.

'What prompted her to go to a cemetery, I cannot imagine. Do you suppose she's planning her own funeral?'

I reminded Val that I had never really met Joyce and couldn't comment on the state of her mind. 'But,' I went on, 'Brookwood is a very interesting place. There was a programme on television about it. I think it's the biggest cemetery in the world or something like that, established during Victorian times because we were running out of space in the graveyards of London. It was set up beside the railway so that bodies could be brought in by rail. They even had special funeral trains.'

'But how would Joyce know about that?'

'There's a sign "Brookwood Cemetery" and the date, which I think can be seen from the train. But here we are.'

Brookwood covers a huge area, about 500 acres and the task seemed enormous.

'Golly!' exclaimed Val. 'Where do we start?'

'Needles and haystacks spring to mind.'

'I've an idea why she may have come.'

'Oh?'

'She's become obsessed with family history. Her latest line was to try to find Uncle Arthur's grave. I remember now she said something about a cemetery and an Oddfellows Plot. Uncle Arthur was an Oddfellow, you see.'

'In what way odd?'

Val laughed. 'The Independent Order of Oddfellows. It's a sort of alternative to the Masons.' We wandered down the main aisles and found the Oddfellows plot, where there were a few monuments; some were quite impressive and the plot was surrounded by trees. 'Good Heavens! There she is! Joyce, you absolute lunatic!'

'Oh, you've found me. Good.'

Her facial features were remarkably similar to those of her sister but she was dressed untidily in an old pale-coloured mac, not quite as long as her skirt, which was the sort of muddy brown that suggested homespun. The mac was pulled close by what appeared to be a length of rope. She was wearing "sensible shoes". I glanced at Val, whose attire was of casual elegance… could it be Armani? Her shoes were stylish, although they did not have high heels. Val's hair was a chestnut colour and perfectly styled; Joyce's was grey and rather untidy.

'I can't find it. I'm sorry if you've had a problem finding me; I lost my phone and couldn't ring you, but I did tell you I was going to come here and when I realised it was beside the railway, I got off. I was going to ask you to come down and join me. But anyway, you're here. And who's this?'

'I suppose you mean you can't find Uncle Arthur's grave, and as to who this is, I would not be here, but ringing up all the hospitals in South East England to try to find you, if it weren't for him. His name's Stuart by the way.'

'Hello, Stuart.' Joyce gave me a little wave of her hand.

'Stuart,' continued Val inexorably, 'picked up your mobile phone that you'd left on the train at Woking. I rang it, to tell you I'd be late for our meeting at Waterloo.'

'Thank you, Stuart.' Joyce again gave me a little wave.

'Why do you imagine Uncle Arthur's grave would be here? I know you've been fretting about its whereabouts for a while now.' Val turned to me. 'Joyce has been doing research into our family history. She's done very well.'

At this I almost expected her to pat Joyce on the head in the manner of a fond grandparent.

'I've never wanted to do my own family,' I said. 'It seems rather pointless and one might uncover skeletons. What was your Uncle Arthur's name?'

'Robinson.' The sisters spoke together.

'Where did he come from?' I asked.

'His father was born in Loughborough,' Joyce offered. 'He was born in London.'

'It's a common name and the whole country is littered with Robinsons. How you can expect to find his grave, I don't know.' Val spoke peremptorily.

'When was he born?' I asked.

'The father, Josiah, in 1867, the son Arthur, who was our cousin really, in 1897.' Val spoke shortly, as though that should be the end of it.

'But he was illegitimate,' persisted Joyce. 'Then he and his mother disappear…'

'Disappear?'

'She means,' Val spoke as though her sister were a small and not very clever child, 'that there is no record of him in the 1871 and 1881 censuses.'

'So that's the father? Josiah, you said?'

'Yes.' Joyce tapped her forehead as though trying to extract information. 'But he appears in 1891 as a policeman with the Metropolitan Police, then as a... what was it, Val?'

'Insurance agent...'

'Hang on.' I was confused. 'How do you know all this?'

'Because she has been wasting all her leisure time and money on digging in record offices all over the country.'

'If I want to do it why is it a waste of time and money and what about your spending money on clothes and that ridiculous gym?' Joyce had suddenly become less passive, although "outburst" would be too strong a word for her interjection.

Margaret, my late wife, and I were... had been... only children and we had not been blessed with any children of our own, so sibling relationships were something of a mystery to me. I only half listened to the sisters' squabble, which continued for a moment or two. I sometimes feel lonely since Margaret died and have wished that I had siblings or children or, at my age, there might have been grandchildren. When I returned to their conversation it had taken a new tack.

'I'll admit,' said Val, 'that it is all quite fascinating, but we know that Josiah married Clare, they had the one kid and that there was some sort of row with our family, though what the relationship between Josiah and our grandmother was we don't know. What can you hope to gain from finding his grave?'

'Well, it might say something about him…'

'You don't know what the relationship between Josiah and your grandmother was? You mean how they got on rather than their familial bonds?' I asked.

'She spoke of Josiah in such a guarded way—' Joyce began.

'"Dear Cousin Arthur" was the usual preface to the rare comments she made about his son though,' interposed her sister.

'So if Arthur… that's the younger one?' I asked; Joyce nodded, '… was a cousin, then Albert, his father, must have been your grandmother's brother? Or great-grandmother?' I was lost; it needed to be written down for me to be able to understand.

'But he is not on the censuses; he must have been sent away,' Joyce spoke earnestly. 'And his mother was Mildred Robinson and—'

'And our great-grandfather married a Mildred Robinson. But,' Val made a chopping motion with her hand, 'but, we cannot prove anything and…'

I disconnected myself from their bickering. It all sounded so complex.

'Look Joyce,' said Val, 'have you any idea about Arthur's grave?'

'I can't see it.' She looked helplessly round.

'It's pointless looking for something unless we at least know that there is something to look for. Where is the office? Look! There is a notice of where things are.'

We found the office and learned that it would take a fortnight for a search to establish if Arthur was buried in Brookwood.

When this was concluded I looked at my watch. 'It's two o'clock and none of us has eaten any lunch. We were all going to be in London this afternoon. Why don't we find a really good restaurant in the West End and have a meal?' I said this in a sort of desperation, to extricate myself from the situation. We made our way to Brookwood Station and within the hour we were at Waterloo. On the train, whilst Val excused herself to go to the toilet, Joyce spoke to me confidentially, almost conspiratorially.

'I know it sounds as though we are at loggerheads all the time, but I really am very fond of Val. She's had a hard life, a brute of a husband who left her when he found she couldn't have children. Although at least with the divorce settlement and her earnings at a fashion design place, she has plenty of money and a nice flat in the West End.'

As we neared Waterloo, Val returned and Joyce stood up. 'I must pop to the loo. Back in a minute!'

Val now spoke about her sister, though not in quite the confidential manner that Joyce had taken. 'Joyce is a lovely person and I am fond of her, but she needs to be, well, protected. She and Colin, her late husband, were very happy and they had, well, have, two delightful sons, Paul and Sam. He, that is Sam, has two children and they all love "Grandmother Grey" as they call her.'

'I suppose she is grey but—'

'It's the children's rhyme our own grandmother taught us:

'Grandmother, grandmother grey,
May I go out to play?
No, no, no, it is a very wet day.

'It goes on a lot more, but I cannot remember it. But here we are, Vauxhall, nearly there and here is Grandmother Grey!'

Joyce seemed less vague now, and Val more light-hearted. Immediately after making the suggestion about a meal in the West End I had regretted it and had been trying to think of a convincing excuse to wriggle out of it, but now I began to think it would be interesting to find out more about this family.

It was a pleasant, relaxed affair in a little Armenian restaurant that Val knew. I never saw the exhibition at Tate Modern, nor got to a play, although I found that Joyce and Val had similar interests to my own.

I made some new friends and we agreed to meet. Eventually, they became almost like my family; Val and Joyce were the sisters that I'd never had, and Joyce's children and grandchildren might almost be my own, though of course I was "Stewie" to Sam and Paul and "Uncle Stuart" to Sam's children. I began to explore my own ancestors' origins, with help from Joyce and Val. A sudden decision to travel up to London, my choosing that seat and Joyce's subsequent choice of seat opposite to me had brought this about. Perhaps the Good Lord had had a plan.

The Strange Tale of Walter Greenhough

Walter Greenhough was frightened of his father and hated his mother. Today he might have been diagnosed as having one of the many syndromes that have been recognised. In the 1940s and 1950s, when he was growing up, his parents and teachers found him "difficult", although perhaps A. S. Neill's adage, "there are no problem children only problem parents", would have been a more appropriate analysis. He was an only child, so had no ready means of relating to others in the home and so withdrew into his shell. At school he remained isolated, unable to relate to the other children.

His father Ralph was one of those men whose behaviour in public was at variance with that within the family. In the pub or the golf club he was a cheery, outgoing man, always ready with a joke; at home he was a stickler for rules.

'Tie your shoelaces properly, boy! Don't toss your hair back like that. Makes you look like a sissy!' Ralph never beat his son, at least physically, but his constant attacking Walter for minor infringements of dress or deportment amounted almost to that. There was little support from his mother, Elizabeth. "Do as your father tells you!" was her favourite maxim.

He managed to pass the eleven-plus, went to the grammar school in the Surrey town where they lived and with his few O levels secured a rather boring job in the offices of the borough council. He loved history and spent much of his time reading various books on the subject which he borrowed from the library. The interest in history prompted him to join the town's history society, where he renewed his acquaintance with Peter Brandon, the chairman of the society, who had taught history at the grammar school. Peter encouraged him and eventually persuaded him to take History A-level examinations. He achieved grade A and Peter suggested that he apply to university. Because he was a mature student, the University of Melcester was prepared to accept him even though he had only one A-level; he knew that Peter Brandon, as his referee, had praised him highly.

In those days there were no tuition fees and students over twenty-one who had worked for a few years were given full maintenance grants. He lived in a hall of residence and because he was a mature student some tutorial duties were offered during term time; in return he was allowed to stay in hall during the vacation. He had no wish to return home and his parents did not seem to want him to. He did keep in touch and even visited them briefly at holiday times, such as Easter and Christmas, when they made polite but stilted conversation or sat in the lounge and watched television. They never enquired about his life at university and he told them nothing about it. Had he been pressed he had a story ready, one of hard study by day and a frenetic nightlife. The former was, more or less true, but for the most part he kept himself to himself. He did join the University Rambling and Climbing Club and enjoyed hikes on Sunday and youth hostelling weekends. In his final year he was even elected to the committee of the club as "Equipment Custodian". He never had a girlfriend but was generally liked by all, even though he was regarded as something of an enigma.

It would be very satisfying to write that after achieving a First at Melcester he undertook research in a key area and had a glittering academic career. In fact he obtained a good second class degree, took the Post Graduate Certificate of Education course and obtained a teaching post in a grammar school in Cleadonbridge in the North of England. He rented a small flat near the town centre where he lived alone.

Just after a rather strained Christmas visit he received a letter from his mother in which she wrote: "We do really need to explain certain things to you, sort things out…" As he had only one bedroom he arranged accommodation for them at a nearby hotel. They did not arrive. A telephone call to their home brought no response. It was the middle of the following afternoon when he learned what had happened. Their car had been involved in an accident on the M1 and both were killed outright.

He felt no real grief; in fact he had almost a sense of relief, as though a weight had been lifted from his shoulders. It took until midsummer for probate to be cleared and his parents' house sold. Walter had decided that he did not want to live there. Having invested the money from the sale of the house in several good schemes, suggested by a local accountant, Walter was able to buy a house in Coldwell, a delightful village about five miles from Cleadonbridge and with a good train service into the city. He was able to buy some furniture and, as it was a seventeenth-century cottage it seemed appropriate that these were antiques. Over the years he was able to add to them. He sold the few pieces he had from his parental home. He wanted a new start.

Once settled in Coldwell he decided to become involved in village life. In retrospect he was never sure why he had not done anything like this before, nor why he wanted to do so now. He joined several village associations, the Local History Society, the Garden Society and the Drama Group; although in this last he only wanted to help backstage. His joining the Garden Society was prompted by the fact that there was a large garden, which was something he had never previously had. His parents' garden was small and such work as was needed was done by his father.

Although he had little or no faith, and his parents had never attended church other than for weddings and funerals, he decided to go to the parish church; neither he nor his family had ever been churchgoers, but it was at the centre of village life and the Church of England did not seem to put many burdens on its members.

'How nice to see you!' A well-dressed and almost flamboyant lady greeted him as he walked up the path for Morning Service on the first Sunday. 'Are you the young man who has just moved into Mrs Armstrong's cottage on Riverside?'

Walter remembered that was the name of the previous owner. 'Yes, I moved in on the 30th of August.'

He knew something of the church liturgy and the Authorised Version of the Bible; part of his degree course had included the religious changes in Britain at the time of the Reformation. The words now said and sung in context appealed to him somehow, although he could not accept the basic premises. What also appealed was the welcome he received in smiles and greetings as he left.

At the door, surplice billowing in the wind, the Rector was fulsome in his salutation. 'My wife Maud tells me you have just moved into Riverside.' So the flamboyant lady was Mrs Rector. Maud. He wondered if one addressed him by his Christian name and what it was. Later he saw that the full name was Herbert Foster, but from others' greetings he realised most called him "Rector".

'Hello!' A young woman, perhaps of sixth-form age, smiled as they left the churchyard, raising her eyebrows in a manner that might have been considered seductive. 'Are you going to the dance in the village hall on Saturday?'

Although it was the 1960s, a place like Coldwell did not "swing". He imagined that the dance would be a fairly staid affair. The school where he taught was all boys but none came from Coldwell as it was in a separate education authority; there was no likelihood of any of his pupils seeing him there. However, it was as well not to become involved with young women here. 'Erm, I'm not sure – I've lots to do… having just moved in, you know.'

As a young unmarried man he attracted attention from the ladies of the congregation. Some of the younger ones considered him attractive, if rather reserved. He had slipped into a village wedding; many who were not invited guests did this. Here he had been struck by the phrase praying that the bride "be a follower of holy and godly matrons". The weekly prayer and Bible study group consisted mainly of such matrons and, though perhaps holy and godly, they were also nosy and asked about his family. Somewhat reluctantly he told them the bare outlines of his recent bereavement, but then he indicated, more by his manner than by words, that he did not want to talk about it. The matrons expressed their sorrow and offered to pray for him. They and indeed most of the village looked on him in a kindly way, orphaned and without any close kin.

'Oh, Mr Greenhough, I'm glad I've caught you!' The speaker was one of these ladies of the parish. She extended her hand. 'Mary Fawcett. It's the church's 750th anniversary next year and we're hoping to update the history. Have you seen the present book?'

He had and was not impressed. 'Yes and err…' he didn't know how to put it.

'Well you'll have seen it has not been updated since Mr Foster came in 1960. Now it is a history and I believe you are an historian.'

'Well it's not my sort of…' He thought quickly. Local history had not been part of his course, nor had he done any documentary studies, but he could have a try. '… OK. I'll try my best.'

A Little History of Our Church had been written in the 1950s and was priced at One Shilling. There were a number of photographs and descriptions of some of the main features of the building, together with various anecdotes, some of which were probably legendary. There was no real structure or historical context, but that was typical of such publications, he supposed. If the stated date of foundation was indeed correct, then it was early thirteenth century. Who was on the English throne at that time? He smiled inwardly; historians were supposed to know all that; indeed he was teaching it to his second-form classes… it would probably be during the minority of Henry III, a rather troubled time in England.

During half-term he found the county record office in Cleadonbridge and explained his mission. The archivist was very helpful and he soon found that there were all sorts of documents relating to Coldwell Church, including an obscure reference to earlier buildings. Over the next few weeks and months he made copious notes. He became very well known to the archivists and he almost felt that one particular table was especially his own. Each time he went to the record office there were people trying to establish their family histories. For the most part he ignored them, muttering about "ancestor worship". His work was, of course, serious research, he told himself. One day a middle-aged couple had taken his favourite table.

'Oh dear I…' He felt quite unreasonably put out and his face must have showed it.

'Sorry!' It was the woman who spoke first. 'Have we taken your place?'

Walter attempted a smile. 'None of the places can be reserved; I'm being unreasonable.'

'We've got back a bit further than we thought we would,' said the man. 'You see it's Dad's 80th birthday and we, me and my sister here, thought we could show him how the line of our ancestors is woven into the history of our village.'

Walter had assumed that they were husband and wife trying to find the origins of the ancestors of their children.

That was the case with one or two he had chatted to. Somehow this sounded more like serious research. 'Which village is that?' he asked.

'Berringmoor,' he replied. This Walter knew to be a village in the northern part of the county.

'Our family have been there,' his sister waved the papers that they had written on, 'for at least 300 years.'

'Well nearly,' her brother put in.

'How incredible,' said Walter. 'I…' He had been about to state that he could not do that as he didn't know where his parents came from, but then he realised that he probably could find that out, but that he didn't want to know; he had "shaken the dust of Surrey off his feet". What was that a quotation from?

'Have you ever thought about doing it?' asked the woman. 'I'm Jane by the way.'

'And I'm Michael,' said her brother.

'Well I hadn't but…' An idea was forming in his mind.

'Well, if you want any help let us know,' she said. 'Our name is Rockingham-Dunne.'

'We're the only Rockingham-Dunnes in the telephone directory,' put in her brother.

'Thanks. I'm Walter Greenhough, but I'd better get on – I am trying to write a history of our parish church in Coldwell.'

'That sounds interesting,' put in Jane. 'You must tell us when it's complete.'

'Greenhough, that's a Lancashire name, isn't it?' asked Michael.

'Is it?' asked Walter. The Rockingham-Dunnes seemed to want to chat, but an idea was forming in his mind. He excused himself and fled to the further corner of the search room. He managed to avoid them for the rest of the session and was relieved that their paths did not cross for a long time. Lancashire? Had his father come from there? He didn't really care but... Walter had never speculated about what his mother had been about to tell him. *We do really need to explain certain things to you, sort things out*; he should have tried to find it out before embarking on his project.

In the record office there was a book in which those searching for ancestors wrote details. One struck him:

> *Please could you fill me in on the Wilfred Sawyer line as this has been a difficult one. I have Janet and George as having 6 Children and married June Qtr 1871 Cleadonbridge. I have Kenneth Sawyer as the father but no mother and 3 siblings for George. Do you have additional info?*

He began to work on an imagined history of love, disgrace and a new beginning. His father, he decided, could have been a younger son of the Earl of Applegate, a place he found in Cheshire. The family name was Greatorix, so he was Ralph Greatorix. He fell in love with one of the servants, Elizabeth Greenhough, but the family could not countenance a marriage of one of their sons with a common serving wench, as the Earl described her. Walter decided that they married secretly and presented the Earl and Countess with a fait accompli. Ralph was disinherited and ordered to leave the house. He had to make his own way, managing to scrape together sufficient money to train as an accountant. He changed his name to that of his wife so that they could live in relative obscurity, far away from Applegate Hall.

Over the next weeks Walter elaborated the fiction and as he developed the story he began to believe it himself and he decided to tell the people at the Bible Study Group the following evening. They were ploughing their way through the first epistle of James and a section which began: *Believers in humble circumstances ought to take pride in their high position.*

'You never know who people are, do you?' put in one of the ladies.

The conversation meandered along far from any deep theological insight, as was usual, and then Maud Foster rose. 'Time for coffee and biscuits, I think. Can one or two of you give me a hand please?'

As the coffee was being poured, Walter spoke. 'You know, Mrs Foster, my situation is a bit like that in that passage.'

'What do you mean, Walter?'

'The high and low positions. You see...' And so he described the romance of Ralph and Elizabeth.

The "godly and holy matrons" listened, entranced; apart from the Rector there was only one other man in the group. Walter found he was enjoying being almost drowned in a wave of sympathy that washed over him.

'Just imagine, you should be living in Applegate Hall with servants waiting on you...'

'Would you have a title? Lord Walter. Imagine. You wouldn't be living in a cottage at Riverside.'

Walter had already looked this up. 'No. I would just be The Honourable Walter Greatorix.'

Had he been a little more perceptive, Walter might have seen that Maud Foster was staring very hard at him.

On his arrival the following week he was greeted in

the hallway by the Rector's wife in a somewhat less than effusive manner. 'I'm glad that you are able to make it tonight.'

'Well thank you, Mrs Foster, I—'

'Roger! He's here now!' A tall man who seemed somehow familiar walked into the hallway of the Rectory. 'This, Walter, is your Uncle Roger.'

The stranger held out his hand and Walter realised that he bore a strong resemblance to his father. 'We never met, but I was, well, let's say… the estranged brother of your father, Ralph Greenhough.'

One Day in the Caff

I've been running my little caff just near the city centre for a long time; yes, I know it's properly a café, I did have an education, but my customers call it Sue's Caff... anyway, I've had it now for, well, it must be nearly twenty-five years. Quarter of a century, gawd help us. I know most of my regulars by name and I've got to know them and their various doings quite well; sometimes they tell me and sometimes I overhear things, things perhaps I wasn't meant to hear. There was a priceless day last week.

Bill, one of my regulars, was the first off the mark as soon as I opens that morning, demanding his bacon and eggs.

'Mornin' Sue! The usual and a pint of tea.' He works at Fergusons, the engineering firm on London Road, toward the airport. He was complaining about the foreman as usual. 'Five minutes before t' shift ended he started us sweepin' up t' workshop. Said it were a disgrace and we weren't any of us goin' home until it were clean!'

I knew what comes next.

'Eeeh, I'm ready for that bacon, love... all t' time waiting for t' bus I were thinking of it and the lovely Sue.'

'Oh, get along do!' I tells him. 'Anyroad, here's your

breakfast. That should shut you up, you and your "lovely Sue". You just read your paper and keep your peace, and don't let page three give you any ideas!' He's not a bad sort is Bill and I know all his chatting up is a pretence. In this business you need to keep the customers happy, so I sort of string along with it.

Soon after that another bloke comes in, in a suit, a bit rumpled and carrying the *Guardian*, not the *Sun*. This shows he's not like Bill or indeed most of the guys who come in here. He's not too certain of himself, and seems weary. Bill, even under his work grime, was a sexy man; this fella seemed rather dull and boring.

He orders bacon, tomatoes and tea, then moves over to join Bill.

'Is this seat free?' he asked.

'Oh aye. Help yourself, mate,' Bill replied. 'Had a hard night?' he asked.

The new guy seems to rouse up at this and grins. 'Yes!'

Bill tells the newcomer about the foreman making them tidy up at the end of the shift. I've heard it all before so I don't pay much attention, but the other guy, whose name's Martyn, explains his situation.

'Oh, that's not the sort of hard night I've had!'

'Eh? Oh I get you, mate! Nice bit of crumpet then?'

Now I like to think of myself as a woman of the world, nothing shocks me, and I was torn between enjoying a bit of a racy story and being rather cross, for they didn't lower their voices.

'Bloody marvellous. Mind you I've not had much sleep!' he leered. 'Then bundled out at 6.30 before her old man gets back from night shift.'

'Where's he work then?' asked Bill.

'Err, well I don't suppose it'd matter to tell you… Fergusons.'

'Bloody hell! What's his name then?'

'Jim… Jim Fisher.'

'Bloody hell! T' foreman! Great… bloody great! While he's been knocking hell out of us, you've been…'

'Knocking hell out of his missus.' To give him his due he was slightly embarrassed.

'Bloody great! You married then?'

'Yes. She's… well… she's attractive. Bloody good looker, but, well, you know how it is. She's just not interested, if you get me… oh, I'm whacked. Anyway, I've only got to survive today. The wife and I are off to Majorca on the five o'clock flight. That gave me the excuse to stay overnight in town – get some work finished on the computer.'

'But what's Mrs Fisher like?' asked Bill.

But he and Martyn bend close together and I can't hear what they're saying. From time to time their belly laughs tell me what they're talking about and I have other customers to serve. Most of them are ordinary enough, order their food, eat it and go, but that day some weird characters comes in. One of them is a youngish woman with clothes that looks as though they might be from great-grandma's cast-offs, though somebody did say tell me such are "ethnic", whatever that might be. She hesitates about her choice so I makes a suggestion.

'I've got some lovely back bacon this morning.' It was as if I'd suggested arsenic.

'Bacon! I'm a vegetarian!'

'Oh... well,' I suggests, 'how about eggs?' And then she asks me if they're free range. I've no idea, and I tells her so, and she starts on at me.

'Do you ever consider the birds? They get stuffed in a confined space with no room to move their legs.'

So of course Master Bill and his new friend Martyn have to join in with the obvious comments about birds and being stuffed and legs.

'I reject all forms of factory farming!' she says, like as if she were preaching.

I tries to calm her down, though I'm seething inside. 'How about cheese on toast?'

She grudgingly accepts that. 'I am hungry. It is breakfast time and I do want it.'

Bill and Martyn picked up on that of course. I'm getting really mad with them and with this customer. For two pins I'd suggest that she leave, but I am in business and the customers have to be right, even when they are wrong.

Then she wants to know if it's wholemeal bread, so I said to her, 'No, it's ordinary white toast loaf,' and she asks if I know what's been taken out of it? This was beyond me. I know brown is supposed to be better for you, but I don't like it and nor do my customers.

'Fibre! Vitamins!' she shouted. 'And once it's out, you can't get it back!' It was almost as if it's a set-up, as it sets those two off again and they're not silenced by me glaring at them.

'No! I must not compromise myself. Ah! Ryvita!'

I asks her sarcastically if that's all. And madam starts going on about "real coffee"; I tells her it's real Nescaff.

'I'll just have water,' she says and goes off into the corner.

The next customer's a thin lady and what happens with my two gents, though "gentlemen" is not a word I'd use about them, anyway, gets me really angry. They're still talking about the shenanigans Martyn had and then one asked if the other fancied this new customer. Loudly enough for her and all to hear he says, 'No I don't fancy her. I've always liked 'em well covered.'

This woman seemed as though she was as picky as the last one. 'Oh dear! Is that all you have?'

It wasn't fair to take it out on her, but I got really sarky. 'You could have Ryvita and water.'

Fortunately she doesn't seem to realise I was being sarky. 'What? Oh, no… no! But I've got to watch my waistline.'

Now she did have my sympathy. 'Counting calories are you?'

'I am. I calculate my diet down to the last calorie. Do you know, I've kept it under five hundred every day since last Thursday?' That really did impress me. 'Could I have one, no one and a half slices of toast, no butter.'

'It's marge, love,' I told her. I think that has less calories, so I thought she might eat it.

'Oh!' she said. She had a little pad with something written down on it and looked at it. I suppose it was the diet plan. 'Well… no better not!'

I really did… what's that word that one of my customers said, not sympathise, empathise. I said to her, 'It's awful isn't it? I know when I've tried to diet, well, everything I wanted to eat was impossible. You know, I used to say, I'll have my diet first and then have my dinner… I don't worry now. He'll have to have me as I am.'

But she said, 'Oh I don't care what men think. I just like to be fit. Health for health's sake. Do you know, I don't want to eat the wrong foods now.'

This amazed me. 'Really?'

'Oh yes. Dry toast and black coffee is all I really want just now.'

'Oh I couldn't do that. No, I don't feel the day's really begun unless I have some nice bacon and toast with butter dripping out of it. I am trying to cut down on sugar in tea.'

'Oh well, that's something,' she says.

'I dote on cream cakes,' I told her.

The she suddenly stops. 'Oh… you know I'm going to…' and it all came out in a rush. 'Can I have some bacon… fat bacon, fried eggs, fried bread, hot buttered toast, jam, tea… and… give me some sugar.'

'That's right!' I told her. 'You really let yourself go! Sit down and I'll bring it to you.' Like I always say, you only live once and if you're worried all the time about what you eat, you can't enjoy your life. Better a short happy one than a long miserable one.

I felt cheered by this, but of course Bill had to start. 'Eeh! She could have that three times a day and she wouldn't be right for me. I like a more comfortable ride. None of your bony ones for me. What I want in a bird is…'

I decides to have it out with him. 'Now listen to me, Bill, and you too, Mister. I don't care what you do outside, or what you talk about in here to yourselves, but I won't have you making remarks like you did when that first lady were here.'

'Nay, Sue. Martyn here were just telling me about last night…'

'I'm not interested,' I told him.

'Hey, but listen, Sue, he were having it off with our foreman's missus, and she's a right hot piece it seems.'

'Well, that's as maybe,' I said, 'but just keep it to yourselves. And anyway,' I said to the other one, Martyn, 'that's no way to speak of your paramour.' I liked that word; I'd read it in a book and had to look it up in a dictionary: "a lover, especially the illicit partner of a married person".

Bill of course didn't understand; he's not an educated man, 'What the bloody hell's a paramour?'

Martyn knew of course; he is educated. 'My lover, mistress, what you will. But honestly Miss… Sue. I don't just think of her as a sex object. I mean she's a… well, I mean she and I have a really good relationship.'

'Well it's none of my business,' I said, but I told him, 'just talk quietly when we've customers at the counter.'

Jim comes in now with his mates from the Cleansing Department. I like them and normally I get on well with them, but this morning he's the cause of me really losing my temper. He gabbles out the order, something like… 'Bacon and eggs twice, one bacon and two eggs, one bacon and sausage, three pints of tea, two with and one without and a coffee with.'

I just says, 'Can you say that again?'

So he gabbles it out, even faster and I says, 'I can't get them down fast enough,' and all the men fall about.

'Now listen to me!' I says. 'I've had just as much as I can stand…'

'All right!' said Bill. 'All right! Come on Martyn lad. Work for you… home to bed for me, not that I'll have as much fun there as when…'

That's that, it seems, and for the rest of the day we've the usual type of people; well, there's no one type, just a lot of different and, well, normally boring people really, and I forget the hoo-hah of the morning. Quite a rush at lunchtime, then a steady stream, many catching the airport bus. At teatime this woman comes in, bit of a sourpuss, I thought. Suitcase, smartly dressed.

'Come on! This'll do fine! Come on do! There isn't much time.'

She's followed by a man I assumes is her husband. He seems familiar but so many people pass through here and I don't really stop to consider when I'd seen him.

'Look here, Elizabeth, I don't think… it's not quite…'

'It's not the Ritz,' said the wife; this annoyed me, such a patronising "b", but the customers are always right so I gave her a smile. 'All I want is a coffee and a scone or something, and the airport bus stops right outside.'

'I don't feel hungry.'

'Well, just have a coffee.'

'I don't feel thirsty.'

'Well I do. You can please yourself. Get me a coffee and cream cake,' she said as she marches in, sits down and starts doing her make-up.

So he follows her in and sidles up to the counter with his head turned away. He looked a bit put upon and I sort of imagined that he must have a crick in his neck or something. 'One, err, no two coffees, milk but no sugar and… a couple of éclairs.'

Of course they don't want sugar, types like that never do; me, I can't take a drink of tea or coffee without it and I suppose I ought to admire them, but I suppose it's daft really I always think that those who don't are rather sourpusses, and she certainly seemed to be.

He now starts sidling up to me making strange movements with his hands, giving me a silly grin.

'Come here!' said his wife. 'What on earth are you doing? I don't mind a little discreet flirtation, but with a woman like that! Really!'

"A woman like that" indeed. She is a "b"! I ignored her and looked at the guy. 'Off on holiday then?'

'Yes… Majorca.'

'Oh very nice,' I says. I felt sorry for him, married to that one. 'I'd say, looking at you, you need a good rest.'

'Yes.' He seems embarrassed, like, and starts making funny signs with his hands again and shaking his head. Off his rocker, I thinks, not surprising with her for a wife.

She now joins in. 'My husband works extremely hard. He is in computers.' She said "computers" as though it was gold and diamonds. 'Yes, he had to work very hard last evening. He had to complete several very important assignments before we had to go away on our vacation.'

'Aye,' I says, 'he looks as if he were at it all night.'

At this the poor chap looks, well, almost suicidal.

'Where is the ladies' room?' demands madam. I points it out to her. She turns to him. 'Pull yourself together, man! You are really behaving in a most peculiar manner.'

Once she was out of the way he comes back to the counter and hisses at me, 'Don't let on, Sue, please!'

'Let on?'

'About last night.'

'Last night?'

'You know... me and Marilyn. Last night? Mrs Fisher... you know... Bill's foreman's wife... you know!'

So it was Martyn; I says to him, 'Oh I knew I recognised you! Couldn't quite place you... we've a lot of customers in here. Oh yes, I remember you. Well, it'd serve you right if I did tell your wife, all the fuss you made here this morning.'

'Please...'

Now I might have spilled the beans when her ladyship got back from the loo, but she had so got up my nose with her high and mighty ways that I decides to let him off the hook. 'Bless you, I won't. Customers have a right to their private lives... anyroad, I can see as you've a lot to put up with. But... shh... your wife's coming back!'

Hurriedly he says, 'Well another coffee then!' He calls to his wife. 'What about you, dear?'

'Yes, why not?' she said. 'I could do with another.'

'And a cake?'

'No, not for me.'

'Just think, a couple of hours and we'll nearly be in sunny Majorca!'

'You're all right now?' she asks him, sarky like.

'Me? I'm fine... fine!'

'Well you were acting most peculiarly.'

'I had a beastly night last night. Working till late and then...' all lovey-dovey he was, precious hypocrite, '... but I'm OK now. Two glorious weeks in the sun... together, darling.'

Even sourpuss was smiling now. If only she knew, but I wasn't going to tell.

'You've been overdoing it. You need that holiday... and promise me, when we get back, you won't need to work like that again. If it can't be done by six o'clock or so, then leave it until the next day.'

'No more late nights, I promise. I'll come home to my dear little wifey.' Bless me, they sits there holding hands like two star-crossed lovers… where did that come from? Somebody said it about somebody… was it in Corrie?

Though she didn't really like that expression. 'Little wifey, indeed!' She said the words and tossed her head, but I could see she wasn't really put out. Least said, soonest mended, as they say, and what the eye doesn't see…

I suppose I hoped for a happy ending for them really, but I should have known the next bit was inevitable. Bill always comes in here about that time on his way to work. 'Afternoon Sue! Tea and toast love.' Then he turns to Martyn. 'Hello! Hello! Hello!' He looks at the wife. 'Is this the little bit of crumpet you've been enjoying…? How are you, Mrs Fisher, Marilyn? Me old mate Martyn's been telling me about your little fun and games last night, and I can't say as I blame him leaving that sourpuss of a wife of his for a lovely lady like you. If I were…'

I think it was the suitcases with their labels that made him realise, so he stopped. 'Hey! You're not… oh bloody hell!'

I didn't know whether to laugh or cry, for all three of them. Bill was the innocent in all this; he'd annoyed me that morning with his comments and he would be coming back to the caff, so I turns and gives him a smile, while the wife drags hubby out, leaving their coffee untasted.

Family Tree Drawn up after the death of Maggie Powell in 1951

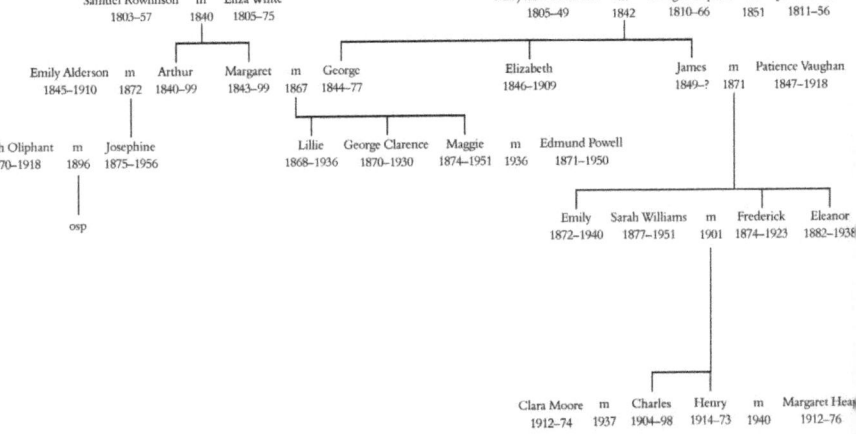

Full family tree established by Angela and Edward.

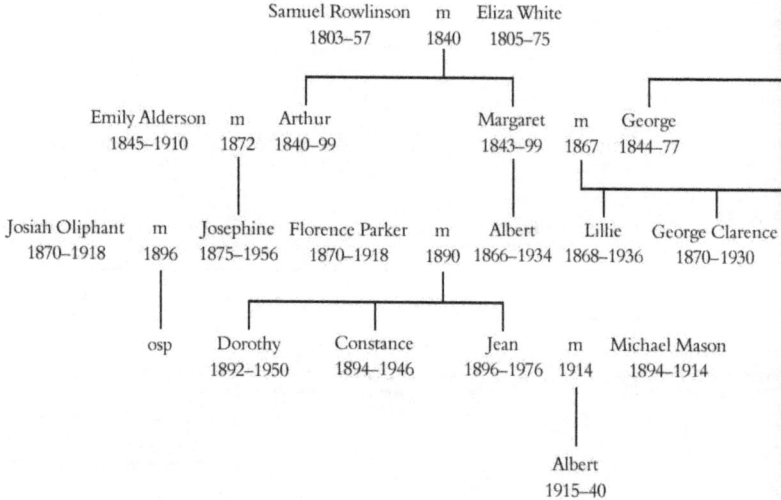

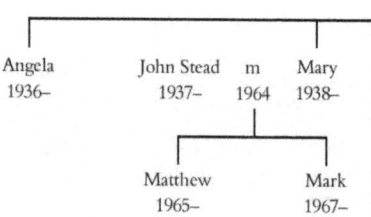

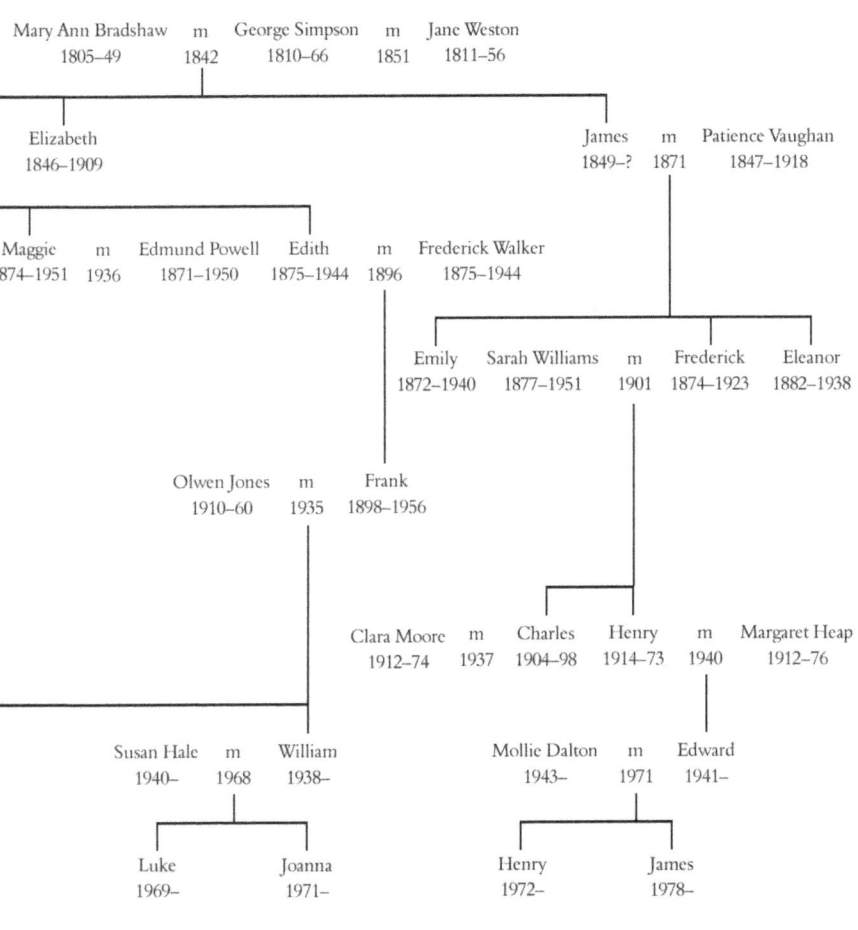

This book is printed on paper from sustainable sources managed under the Forest Stewardship Council (FSC) scheme.

It has been printed in the UK to reduce transportation miles and their impact upon the environment.

For every new title that Matador publishes, we plant a tree to offset CO_2, partnering with the More Trees scheme.

For more about how Matador offsets its environmental impact, see www.troubador.co.uk/about/